FLYING INTO FIRE
BY IVY HANSEN

Book Cover by Ivy Hansen

Published by Ivy Hansen

ISBN: 979-8-218-48531-3

https://www.youtube.com/@catonahampsterwheel

Table of contents

Prologue   6
Chapter One   10
Chapter Two   15
Chapter Three   22
Chapter Four   28
Chapter Five   34
Chapter Six   38
Chapter Seven   51
Chapter Eight   56
Chapter Nine   60
Chapter Ten   65
Chapter Eleven   68
Chapter Twelve   73
Chapter Thirteen   78
Chapter Fourteen   84
Chapter Fifteen   89
Chapter Sixteen   97
Chapter Seventeen   101
Chapter Eighteen   106
Chapter Nineteen   112
Chapter Twenty   118

Chapter Twenty-One   125
Chapter Twenty-Two   132
Chapter Twenty-Three   139
Chapter Twenty-Four   144
Chapter Twenty-Five   152
Chapter Twenty-Six   162
Acknowledgements   169

For my Brothers, Ender, Indie, Adler, and Otto

Prologue

Nevia slipped through the palace, her cloven feet barely touching the ground. The cool feeling of the marble tiles seemed to hint that reality was struggling to keep pace with what was seen. The grand and usually lively hall, which had been the center of so many parties and joyous speeches, was now shrouded in silence. This was a side of the royal family that Nevia alone saw. She hated darkness, so it was a shame she had spent so much time in it. It was past midnight, and Queen Indigo's guards, along with most of the servants, had already gone to sleep. This was her least favorite part of being the Queen's seer. She hated the terrible visions late at night, and the horrible silence of the palace after dark. Thunder clapped in her ear, a flash cutting across her peripheral vision.

A splatter of blood, a young Avian, trapped and wounded, her Queen lying dead on the floor. Sitting in a tree, desperately trying to comfort a broken girl.

Nevia stumbled forward, clutching her head like she was trying to shield her thoughts from invisible eyes. Her vision was going white, bright stars clouding her mind until she could barely tell her thoughts from sight.

I can't let this be my future, she thought desperately, screams still ringing in her ears. She struggled to her feet, head still pounding. A light tear trickled from her left eye, shining off her dark skin like a diamond. She wished she didn't have to see this. It was just a curse she didn't ask for, a cruel twist of fate.

As she stumbled through the darkness, she eventually reached the door, although she wasn't sure she wanted to. Knocking softly on the entrance to Queen Indigo's chambers, she once again noticed the majesty of it. The door was gorgeous, with rubies and sapphires studded along the edges. A large carving of a golden dragon was on the front, with brilliant black eyes of polished onyx inlaid in the golden scales. It seemed too perfect, almost fake. She hated it.

"Your Majesty?" She whispered, careful not to wake the counselor sleeping just two rooms over. Her hand was shaking violently, the panic from the dream mixing with the fear of the Queen's reaction. The ornate decorations could barely be seen in the dim candlelight, and Nevia thought it was a shame so much wealth was tucked away here in the inky black.

"What is it!" Queen Indigo growled, flinging the colossal doors open with a majestic sweep of her talons.

The Queen's dark black hair flowed down her pale back in perfect waves, making her look almost statuesque. Her face was gaunt, pulled back almost like stretching leather over a canvas, and Nevia thought she could see the backs of her eyes right through the skin and bone. Her powerful ruby tail swished back and forth, covered slightly by the dark blue and purple robes tied with a velvet sash.

"I was granted a message from the stars," Nevia said, wishing she could just talk without sounding all mysterious.

She had been in this role so long that even her speech had slipped into cryptic mutters.

"Was it so important you had to wake me up?" the Queen growled.

Nevia nodded quickly, anxiety building with every passing second.

"Come in," The Queen commanded with a flick of her tail.

Nevia didn't like the suspicion layered in Her Majesty's voice. She still remembered the story of the Queen's last seer, who was executed shortly after delivering the prophecy of the king's death. She didn't like to imagine what the Queen would do to her after hearing this. Nevia glanced up, head pounding as she imagined the possibilities.

"I said come in," she said, the welcoming tone somehow worse than a menacing one.

"Yes, Your Excellency," she replied, drawing in a shaky breath.

"So, what was this?" the Queen asked, sitting in a silk-covered armchair in the corner of the room. "Vision of yours?"

Nevia began to speak before she could stop herself. "I saw a boy in flaming blue, still a child but wise beyond his years. The name, Callax Trent, a single glittering blade. He will slay you in your own home, leaving the avians to rule your empire for centuries."

Nevia trailed off, her cryptic tone making the news even worse. Her heartbeat was pounding in her ear, drowning out the rest of her thoughts.

"The Avians?" the Queen demanded. "I got rid of them a long time ago."

"I don't, well," Nevia stuttered. "I just tell you what I've seen."

The Queen didn't speak, keeping her black eyes locked on Nevia.

"What are you going to do?" Nevia whispered, her voice echoing through the silent halls of the palace.

The Queen grinned, her sharp canines glittering in the pale candlelight. "It's quite simple. This boy will not make it to the palace. I'll make sure of that. And in the meantime, I'll keep extra good track of all the Avians in the kingdom. After all, the last thing we need is somebody ruining my perfect world.

Chapter One

Callax Trent

Callax sat in the passenger seat of the car, his gaze fixed on the world outside. Rain was dripping down from the clouds like poison, thumping against the ground and coating the road in water. Callax buried his head in his sleeve, ignoring the crackling storm. He didn't hate rain; he hated what it reminded him of. What he couldn't seem to forget. It had only been three weeks since the rain had poured like a tidal wave, drowning out the sounds of the bombs. Only three weeks since the terrible night he had been pinned under that flagpole, hearing the screams of the people he loved and unable to do anything about it. The night he thought would be his last.

Callax reached down to touch his new prosthetic, feeling a fresh wave of despair at the sight of the silver metal. It was almost unbearable, but he refused to make a sound. The last thing he wanted to do was cry, not around Mrs. Kinnian, who was far too pleased considering the current situation. Her overall demeanor was shockingly bright, from her blond hair to her neon yellow cardigan, her entire appearance screamed friendly. Callax was surprised he hadn't gone blind. She was on the larger size, her face blushed like a cherry tomato. Her horns, the only thing on her that looked even close to aggressive, had been beveled at the ends like she smoothed them over with a nail file.

For someone who works with traumatized children, you seem oddly chipper. He thought wryly. He was almost positive this lady hadn't had a bad day in her life. Whoever hired her probably had the best intent, but Callax didn't really care at this point.

"WE'RE HERE!" Mrs. Kinnian exclaimed cheerfully, her face even brighter with the street light illuminating her spray tanned skin.

Callax abruptly sat up, fixing her with a sharp glare.

Mrs. Kinnian's warm smile dropped, worry crossing her face for the first time all trip. "Are you okay, dear? I promise Uncle Trent is really quite nice," she soothed. I know it won't be the same, but he's your family, too."

Callax felt a stab of guilt. *It's not her fault.* He thought, tail curling beside him into a flickering coil. But he couldn't quite bring himself to be any more polite with all the thoughts clouding in his head. His parents had always told him to be grateful. He had tried that, but he only thought about home. His real home, away from the hospitals and social workers. And he really wanted people to stop telling him it would be okay.

"I'm fine." He murmured, pulling out the nicest expression he could manage. "Thank you for the ride."

"That's great, dear. Do you need some help getting inside?" She briefly glanced down at the silver prosthetic below his knee, causing Callax to shrink back into his seat. He didn't want to be *that* kid.

"No, that's alright." Callax opened the car door, the sun barely peeking over the dispersing clouds. He stepped onto the rough pavement, surprised at how easy walking was. The artificial leg was hardwired with all kinds of tech to the point that it functioned almost identically to the original. That still didnt fix much though. It was a tiny fleck of silver on the pile of awfulness life just dealt him. He reached behind the seats and grabbed his tattered green and blue duffel bag. Hoisting it over his shoulder, he ambled up the polished stairs to the door of his Uncle's house and into the hall.

~

The place was huge, almost five times the size of his old home. If he hadn't known better, he could have mistaken it for the palace itself. The walls were pure oak wood; he could make out little shapes that resembled flames etched into the smooth tile flooring. His Uncle's status as the Queen's top general earned him a small fortune, and he obviously lived like a king because of it. Callax turned to the desk, seeing a pale man wearing a tidy suit. He bore an uncanny likeness to him, the same flickering blue eyes and flaming tail. This man had to be his Uncle, looking almost exactly how Callax imagined himself in 30 years.

Except Uncle looked broken. Not on the outside, he was taller than most and quite handsome for his age. But his face was so pale, not even close to Callax and the rest of his family. He lacked the strong arms and broad shoulders most of Callax's relatives had, which was a result of the many strict hours in the forges. He clearly had spent most of his days inside, lacking the distinctive tan of a Trent. Uncle looked clearly related to Callax's dad, but he had none of the warm certainty that seemed to radiate from father. Father always smelled like roasted marshmallows, and his strong golden eyes made everyone around him feel safe. Uncle's eyes felt almost wrong, and the light blue flames reminded Callax of melting ice.

"Who are you?" Uncle rasped from his place behind the desk.

Callax kept his eyes on the floor, sliding the hospital letter towards his Uncle with shaking hands.

He unwrapped the letter, reading over the words printed out in arial bold. The paper was crisp and technical, and it made Callax's chest hurt to see the circumstances laid out so simply. Those words represented the rest of his life, and they hadn't even bothered to change the basic font.

His Uncle finished reading, setting the letter facedown on his desk. His usually pale skin turned sheet white, and the flames in his eyes grew until they almost looked like he was burning from the inside.

"I was told you didn't survive the bombing," He said quietly, tail flicking tiny embers on the desk.

"I did…"

"What about my brother?"

"He didn't make it" Callax felt the small flame on his tail flaring up, leaving burns on his Uncle's once-perfect floor. "Um, I'm sorry."

Uncle looked him over, expression twisted into a gruesome frown.

"You can stay in the room upstairs." His Uncle was glancing from side to side as if his nephew's presence would send bombs coming from the ceiling. "You have school first thing in the morning."

Callax bowed awkwardly, rushing up the stairs before his Uncle could say another word. He didn't want to spend another minute in this place. Not with Uncle. Callax spent the rest of his day searching for a little bit of his old optimism and wishing he was anywhere but here.

Chapter Two

Dakota Orio

Dakota's wings flared, and his large feathers knocked down the portrait on the edge of the Headmaster's desk. Sculk dripped off his face, leaving a starry purple goo all over the once-clean floor. The office was covered in stains from the many times he had lost his temper after getting in trouble. He sometimes wished emotions weren't so messy, but ruining stuff with just his feelings was occasionally useful.

"How many times have I told you to control your emotions when you're in my office!" The Headmaster growled, commanding voice thundering through the room. "You're getting your wretched Avian sludge all over!"

The Headmaster's red tail lashed dangerously, sending her paperwork flying across the room. She was standing over him, a stern expression on her gaunt face. Her chestnut hair was pulled back in a tight bun, and her eyes were completely black in the dim room. Her dark skin was even darker in the pale light, contrasting vibrantly against her cream uniform. She was a Peregrine, no surprise there; almost all of the positions of power in the city were held by Peregrines, including the Queen herself.

"Maybe you should stop calling me to your office, then!" Dakota yelled, trying to match her furious gaze. He didn't try to stop the spread of the sculk, allowing his emotions to rise, making the celestial ooze creep over his wings and pour onto the polished floors.

"Stop causing trouble and you won't be in my office!" she spat, claws inches from his face.

"Arox hit my sister!" he squawked indignantly. "I was just defending her! Besides, he wasn't even hurt; it was just a centipede!"

"You should have come to me with a formal complaint instead of putting centipedes in another student's backpack!" she glared at him, black pupils narrowing to angry half-slits. "You need to learn your place! I bet your pathetic little sister deserved it!"

"How could you! " Dakota challenged, the sculk spreading down his leg and staining his brown shorts a midnight blue. His sister Willow was so genuinely kind to everyone. She absolutely did not deserve to be picked on, not now, not ever. He would NEVER let someone hurt her or anyone else in his flock and get away with it.

"And besides, I did tell you the first three times this jerk harassed her, and you didn't do anything!" Dakota snarled. "Just because he's the queen's nephew doesn't mean he should be allowed to act like this!"

"You watch your tongue!" She hissed, unable to come up with a clever argument. "One more violation, and I'll send you to the outer provinces with the rest of your kind!"

Rage almost blinding him, he flicked a handful of sculk at her well-ironed skirt. Flashing her one sarcastic smile, he turned to stalk out of the room, wings flared out behind him.

The Headmaster grabbed his wrist and yanked him back to face her. Her face was twisted in rage, small wisps of black hair drifting out of her tight bun.

"You can't leave yet." She snarled, pulling him by the collar of his shirt. She had a long pair of leather straps and a buckle sharp and metal in her right hand.

Dakota hated that thing. The Headmaster had made the leather binding after he'd shown almost no reaction to her previous forms of punishment. Detention, no problem. Extra homework, piece of cake. Cleaning the halls after school, why not. He was immune. But those binds were worse than everything else combined. She was holding something so simple, but it represented everything he hated. She dug her claws into his feathers, tying the rough leather around his wings. The metal buckle drove into his side, and he could feel the fragile bones in his wings bending at unnatural angles. Of course, the pain was just a side effect that Dakota was all too happy to accept; the real point was to take his wings from him. To ground him, make him nothing more than a small kid, short, light, and useless. He felt trapped, all his instincts screaming to fly away, but he couldn't. He just had to stand here, the old fear starting to creep back into his mind. Having his wings folded so strangely made him terrified of heights. Or more so, falling. He could almost imagine plummeting from the roof, flailing desperately, one last foolish attempt at flight. Hitting the ground, dark eyes relishing his fall. Willow- all alone, having to watch.

She smiled down at him, so pleased with what she'd done that it made Dakota want to tear down the world. The look was so condescending that it made him want to burn the school to the ground and hurt everything until people understood.

This isn't right. Dakota thought, the skulk dripping into his eyes as his emotions flared. He felt violated, like he was just some problem she was trying to sweep under the rug. *She's so wrong. I can't; she can't get away with this.*

"You're only mad because you can't prove me wrong." He blurted.

She smacked him hard, leaving a small red welt on his pale cheek. His face stung, sculk mixing with the red on his face.

"Get out of my office," she demanded, shaking the sculk off her hand.

I was right. Dakota thought with a bit of joy despite his stinging face. *She ran out of words. I win.*

He bowed mockingly, shooting her one last sarcastic grin before disappearing behind the door.

~

Dakota was immediately tackled by a tiny ball of white feathers. The little Avian wrapped her arms around his neck, soft skin buried in layers of thick sweater.

"Dakota!" Willow cried, her face laced with worry. "Are you alright?"

He smiled. "I'm okay, Wil." He instantly felt better, and just seeing his sister's face made him believe everything was worth it. She was his family, really his only family between the banishment and his father's long work hours. Her brown eyes were so kind, and he was convinced she could make anyone happy just by looking at her. Today was one of the rare instances he could see her eyes, as she almost always hid behind her nearly floor-length hair. It was honey blonde and completely straight, almost like a curtain. She wore a light yellow sweater with maple leaves painted on the huge sleeves, most likely something she had drawn while sitting in class. Willow could paint almost anything, and she could paint it well.

"You don't need to keep doing that, you know," she said, voice cracking.

"Doing what!" Dakota said back cheerfully.

"Getting in trouble for me! I can handle a little bullying." she chirped, brown eyes wide.

"I know you can handle it, but you shouldn't have to," he said, smiling at her. "We're a flock, that means we take care of each other. I know you would do the same for me."

Her face softened, wrapping her wings around her older brother.

"You're right." Willow sighed. "Thanks for sticking up for me."

~

Mrs Schultz had been talking for hours, her monotone voice a dull droning. Dakota thought he would die of boredom; biology class sounded more like a personal attack than a lesson.

"This is in sharp contrast to the Avians." Mrs. Schultz continued, glancing down at her lesson plans. "The creatures are chaotic and stupid, and most were sent to work the factories in the outer provinces after the Queen decided they could possibly be a danger due to their uncontrolled spirit and inferior nature. You can always tell when one is upset or excited, as they exude sculk from their skin and eyes when their emotions rise. Thanks to our Queen's brilliant ideas, these inferior beasts now use their limited knowledge to produce the parts necessary for everyday life."

Dakota rolled his eyes, tuning out the lesson. He tried not to mind that the whole class was staring at him. He had heard it all before, so why hear it again? They never gave a reason he was supposedly so inferior. He was lucky his dad worked in the palace, or he would be stuck making toothpaste caps or something else pointless for the rest of his life. He stared at the clock, slowly watching the hours tick by.

After many agonizing lectures, it was 11:30, and it was finally time for lunch. Next to Mrs. Schultz was a tall Deroian about Dakota's age with pale scars running across his tan skin. He was wearing a white shirt with an unzipped blue jacket and denim jeans, and he looked like he was forcing a smile. Dakota saw a small bit of metal peeking out from under the edge of his jeans, and his left shoe looked like it didn't fit quite right. He was clearly a new student, one of the stupid hi, my name is badges plastered to his shirt. It looked like it said Callax, so probably some kid from a village, judging by the spelling. Some of the bigger guys were whispering near the back of the classroom, probably being jerks about something or other. He recognized one of them, a large Peregrine in a puffer coat. He had gotten pinned to his locker by that guy plenty of times, and no doubt this country kid would make an easy target. Callax probably wouldn't even make it to the lunchroom today unless someone decided to be decent. Besides, it would be pretty fun to tell the Headmaster that he had done a better job showing the new student around than her. The bell rang, and the halls were suddenly full of people. He made up his mind, hopping over to Callax, standing by the door and watching the crowd with a worried expression.

"Hey, I'm Dakota." he chirped, skulk beginning to creep up his wings. "Do you want some help finding the cafeteria?"

Chapter Three

Willow Orio

"Your incompetent brother is late," Tempest muttered to Willow. His face was twisted into a perpetual scowl, as it was most days. He was wearing a well ironed green jacket that cost more than Willow's entire closet, the cuff lined with expensive fur. His canine features were even more pronounced in the artificial light, silver hair combed over his neck in perfect strands. His large wolf-like ears were perked like he was listening to something far away, and his tail was sweeped to the side to avoid dragging on the dirty floor. He was a distinguished member of the royal guard, or at least that's what he liked to tell people. Dakota thought Tempest was more of a capitol lap dog.

Willow kicked him under the table, sculk flaking on her face like tiny freckles.

"What was that for!" he cried indignantly, reaching over to touch his knee with a wince.

"My brother is not incompetent." she said, frustrated, both at him for saying something like that and at herself for losing control.

Willow breathed deeply, trying to get the last of the sculk to dissipate. She looked at the table with a stab of distress mixed with empathy for the poor janitors, who, if this was anything like helping Dakota clean his room, would be fighting to get the stain out all afternoon. She was getting better at controlling her emotions, an endeavor her brother thought was a waste of time. He loved seeing the helpless rage on the headmaster's face when he "accidentally" left another stain on her perfect school. She couldn't agree, though. Emotions were just too messy, at least for her. Pearl looked over at them, trying to hide her smirk. She was playing with her clamshell necklace and looked like she had just been swimming.

"Uh huh," Tempest said halfheartedly, tail twitching irritably. "Lucky for no one but you, It sounds like Dakota's on his way."

There was a crashing sound, followed by at least two teachers yelling. Pearl smothered her face in her sleeve, failing to hide her giggles. Willow bit her bottom lip, anxiety already building in her chest. Her brother didn't need any more trouble; people hated them for existing, so why give them more reasons? The cafeteria doors flung open, and Dakota rushed over, a boy she had never seen before running after him.

"Hi everyone." Dakota squawked breathlessly, his bound wings covered almost entirely in sculk. "This is Callax, and he's sitting with us!"

Tempest's ears flattened to his gray hair, a low growl building in his throat. "No one told me about this! The last thing we need is another Dakota."

"He looks nothing like Dakota." Pearl pointed out, earning a sharp glare from Tempest. "I think we should get to

23

know him. If you don't like it, you can sit with your searcher friends."

"Why are you even here?" Dakota chirped, a smirk flickering across his face. "You hate me even more than you hate the rest of the world.

"My friends are absent today," Tempest muttered. "And I couldn't find another table. Don't get too excited; this is a one-time thing."

"Callax, you can sit here." Pearl smiled, gesturing to the seat next to her.

They sat down, and Dakota let out a little chirp of delight. Willow couldn't help but be happy about his enthusiasm. Dakota just seemed excited to be sitting at a full table for once.

"So," Pearl inquired, glancing at the thick bands pinning her brother's wings. "Whatcha you do this time?"

He shrugged, a touch of sculk dripping off his hand. "Arok was being a jerk again, so I might have put just a few centipedes in his backpack, and the Headmaster decided to get all offended when I pointed out she was wrong."

"Dakota!" Willow cried, desperately trying to push back the sculk creeping over her right shoulder. "Why would you antagonize her? For the love of everything, keep out of trouble!"

"She deserved it!" he shot back. "If I don't tell her how stupid she's being, no one else will."

Tempest barked a laugh. "Do you think the headmaster will ever take your advice seriously? You are not only an Avian, but you're the worst student in the entire world."

"What's wrong with being an Avian?" asked Callax, puzzled.

"No one will ever give me a good reason," Dakota complained, failing to mask his annoyance.

"Well, I only know two of them," Tempest said, flicking his tail towards Dakota and Willow. "But if they are anything like Dakota, I can a hundred percent see what's wrong with them."

"And if they are anything like Willow," Pearl snapped back. "Then they are probably the nicest people you could ever meet."

Willow smiled at her friend, glad she had someone to rely on. Pearl was the only person, besides her hurricane of an older brother, who seemed to genuinely like her. Willow stayed out of trouble, so others were polite, but no one else was like Pearl. Pearl had never once called her inferior or judged her for anything less than her character. Willow was so glad to have a best friend and hoped her brother would find someone to spend time with. She peered at Callax, wondering if he would become a permanent part of her ragtag little friend group. He looked worried about something and kept peering down at his left leg as if expecting it to disappear.

"So," Willow started, hoping to help Callax's nerves. "Where are you from?"

Willow suddenly regretted her words, his anxious expression making her hands prick like cacti.

. "I lived in a village near the northern border," Callax said quietly.

"That's really far away," Pearl said, clearly not seeing the worry on his face. "Why did your parents move all the way to the capitol?"

"Th-there was an accident," he murmured, anguish sparking in his fiery blue eyes. "I, um- I don't really wanna talk about it."

A dark silence fell over the group. Willow couldn't even breathe as the tsunami of emotion threatened to drown her. She fought down the swelling sculk under her arms, pressing her wings against her back to look as small as possible.

"I'm so sorry." Pearl blanched. "I had no idea."

"It's okay," he said, shooting a melancholy smile in her direction. "I'm trying to make the best of it."

"Hey guys," Dakota interjected, trying to lighten the mood. "Willow and I were gonna go get something to eat and then head to the abandoned falconry track after school. Do you guys wanna come?"

"That sounds fantastic!" Pearl said enthusiastically, clapping her hands together.

"Sure," Callax said, glancing over at Pearl.

"Fine," Tempest muttered loudly. "But I don't know how you'll fly around that useless track with your wings bound. You'll just fall off the platform and die. Which might be a plus, all things considered."

"The headmaster will unbind my wings before dismissal, right?" Dakota squawked sharply. "If she forgets, I won't be able to fly all weekend!"

"I'm sure she won't forget." Willow soothed, cooing lightly. "And if she does, father could probably get it off."

Tempest rolled his eyes. "What's the big deal? You scared, little birdie?"

"NO!" Dakota snarled, Sculk dripping onto the table. "And I am not a little bird!"

"Sure." Tempest scoffed. "Keep telling yourself that.

"See you guys there?" Willow asked quickly, trying to change the subject before her older brother started a fistfight with a guy who could snap his neck like a chopstick.

Pearl slung her arm over Willow's shoulder. "Oh, of course!" she exclaimed. "Wouldn't miss it for the world!"

Chapter Four

Callax Trent

Come on!" Dakota yelled, diving and flipping in the cold air.

Callax smiled, pleased at how the day was going. The falconry court was incredible, and it seemed a shame it was shut down. But it was still a good time. They were all heading back so Callax could grab some money from his Uncle's house.

Uncle's house. He thought with a wince. *I really need to stop calling it that. It's my home too.*

"So, how do you like the capital so far?" Pearl asked, shaking the lakewater out of her matted brown hair. Her face was blushed with exertion, and her green eyes were almost glowing with enthusiasm. Her jean shorts were soaked through, making the color nearly black. She was wearing an orange shirt, the words *North Star Swim Team* plastered in bold white letters.

"It's nice." He responded, her contagious happiness making him feel all warm inside. "I miss my hometown, of course, but you guys are great, and I have a perfect view of the castle from my bedroom window."

"I'm glad you're happy," Willow said, a smile spreading across her kind face. Callax could hardly believe someone so gentle could be related to rash, impulsive, and overall insane Dakota. Not that he wasn't awesome; he totally was, but Callax couldn't deny that the Avian was a little different. Plus, Callax would never get the stains out of his shirt, which now looked a little less white and a little more like it had been dyed in sparkly blueberry juice.

Dakota swooped out of the sky and perched on Callax's shoulder, digging in his sharp talons. He faltered for a second, wondering if he could hold him up without the strength in his left leg, but Dakota was extremely light. He was much shorter than Callax, and the little Avian boy probably couldn't tip the scales at 60 pounds while soaking wet. Callax bet it was some sort of Avian quirk like their bones were hollow or something like that. He glanced up, spying the dark spruce pillars of Uncl-his house in the distance.

"Sorry about the stop," Callax said, stuffing his hands in the pockets of his jeans.

"You're fine." Dakota chirped, leaping off his shoulder and onto Pearls. "We'll just wait for you outside the door for you to run in and grab your things."

"Sounds good," Callax replied, starting up the driveway.

~

Callax creaked the door open, spotting three searchers gathered around his desk. Uncle was on the phone, shoulders hunched in like he was trying to hide himself.

"Yes, he's staying here." Uncle whispered into his phone. "How long?

Callax walked tentatively past his Uncle's desk, hoping he wouldn't be noticed. He really didn't want to look at those melting eyes.

Uncle Trent placed the phone down on the desk, his face cracked with gruesome expressions.

"I didn't hear you come in." His Uncle glanced up, and Callax noticed a hint of suspicion or maybe even fear in his Uncle's harsh tone.

"I won't bother you," Callax muttered, keeping his eyes on the floor.

"Fine." He said, nails digging into the wooden desk. "Just let me work."

Callax crept up the stairs, wondering why his Uncle was always acting so on edge. Was it just him, or was something really wrong with his estranged relative? And what were searchers doing here? He knew Uncle was a general, but it was still odd. Pushing that thought away, Callax entered his room, looking for his duffle bag. He knew he was supposed to be unpacked already, but yesterday was a little too grim to be worried about how to store his things. The moon was full, bathing the castle in an iridescent sheen. The view was inedible, a silver lining to a sucky situation. He dug around in the bag until he found a small ziplock with about 20 dollars in it. He turned to leave when the spruce door creaked open. The three searchers walked in, visors drawn over their eyes. They were wearing perfectly ironed jumpsuits, the large belts loaded with all kinds of weapons. Callax had seen the uniform before, similar to the outfits of the overseers who patrolled his village. They were holding silver guns, ammo loaded into the barrel. Callax saw a silencer on the gun, which didn't help Callax's nerves in the slightest.

"What are you doing up here?" Callax asked, backing away. "My Uncles downstairs. Does he know you're here?"

"He knows." the searcher in front replied snidely. "We have a bit of business to take care of."

"Can you wait a sec?" Callax asked, sweat beading on his face. Something about how they were standing in front of the door made him nervous.

"Nice try, rebel." the searcher spat, grin shifting into an annoyed frown. "You're not going anywhere."

He fired his gun, a silver bullet piercing Callax's chest. Callax felt his breath catch as he crumpled to the floor, blood splattering in his blue eyes.

"Wh-why Wh-" Callax sputtered, voice cutting off like an old cassette tape that had been paused.

"Just following orders," he replied, wiping a splatter of blood off his helmet. He shoved his gun into its holster, ears flat against his champagne hair. "I'll tell your Uncle you said hi."

The searchers stalked out the door, careful not to get blood on their leather boots. Callax could hear their voices from outside the door, along with his Uncle's panicked murmur. Callax wanted to eavesdrop, but all he could hear was the ringing in his ear. It felt like he was being burned alive, wildfires fraying his nerves like scorched rope. His tail started to flicker out, blue sparks becoming more and more sparse with every breath.

I don't want to die! I'm not ready! Callax thought desperately, clinging to the last of his hope. He remembered a boy from his village, found dead in his garden. He had shot himself, losing all his will to live at just 12. His older sister did the same 3 months later. The night of the funeral, Callax remembered his father holding him, repeating the same desperate words over and over.

They were too young to die. They threw it all away. Wasted.

The words sounded less like a statement than a plea. A plea that his son would never be the one in that casket.

Callax knew exactly what people would think when they found his body. It probably wouldn't even be surprising. After that bombing, most would be done. Ready to end it all. No shocker, the traumatized orphan gave up. It was expected. But Callax couldn't bear the thought of being remembered that way.

I co-could wri-write a note. Callax's mind whispered. *So that at least someone knows what happened.*

Callax could feel the atmosphere getting thicker, air choked by death and blood. He reached for his duffle bag, quickly fumbling out a pen and paper. The world was fading fast from his sight as he struggled with the letter. His throat tightened with every breath, and in the end, he was only able to write one word before passing out.

-Shot

Chapter Five

Dakota Orio

"What's taking him so long?" Tempest grumbled.

"Don't be upset." Willow stuttered, her long strawberry-blonde hair shining in the night air. She was fiddling with the paintbrush in her pocket, a rare bit of sculk showing under her huge sweater.

Dakota peered at the dark house, a foreboding feeling sending sculk creeping over his left arm. There was something peculiar about the brown walls. The place looked both well-kept and uninhabited at the same time. He had a bad feeling about Callax being alone in that house with Mr. Trent. He didn't trust the Queen's goons by default, and Mr. Trent was the one who had carried out the Queen's banishment of the Avians. Dakota had Mr. Trent's picture hanging from his dartboard at home, which Willow kept trying to throw away. It was treason, of course, to defile images of the Queen or her workers, but Dakota thought it was worth it. Mr. Trent deserves everything that has ever gone wrong in his life and more. He still remembered Willow crying in her room, terrified that someone would take them away. He hoped that was the only thing making her so nervous. When she let people see sculk at all something was usually amiss. She usually never let her emotions get past the barriers in her head. He wanted to wrap her in his wings, shutting out all the bad memories and ghost stories.

Pearl looked down at her watch. "It's been almost 20 minutes."

"What if he's hurt!" Willow cried, on the verge of tears. "What if something awful happened!"

"He's fine." Tempest rolled his eyes. "It's more likely he decided he never wanted to see your face again and ran off."

Dakota felt rage start to burn in his mind, sending his emotions ablaze. "DON'T EVER TALK TO MY SISTER LIKE THAT!"

"FINE!" Tempest yelled back. "My point was that nothing's wrong."

Pearl was barely containing her smile like she thought Dakota getting into fights was the funniest thing in the world. She clearly hadn't noticed the fear in Willow's milky eyes, or she wouldn't think it was so amusing.

"He just needed to do the dishes or something." Pearl shrugged nonchalantly.

Dakota didn't think so. He had learned better than to doubt his sister's instincts.

"I'm going to go check on him," Dakota announced.

"I'll go knock on the door." Pearl walked up, her swamp-tinted hand just inches from the wood.

"NO!" Willow screamed, tears streaming down her face.

"Okay, okay!" Pearl backed away, hands up.

"I'll fly up to the window and have a look around," Dakota replied hastily, willing to do anything to calm her down.

Willow grabbed his wing, sculk showing on her face for the first time in forever.

"Please don't go up there," she whispered, wiping the sculk off her face. "Please, don't leave me alone here. Not with him."

"Who?" he asked, unsure if she was talking about Mr. Trent, Tempest, or even the house itself."

"Them," she replied, voice muffled by fabric. "In the house."

He thought his heart might just snap in half. He didn't want to go anywhere near that window, closer to all the nightmares. And he definitely didn't want to leave Willow alone, but if she was right and Callax was in trouble, he had to do something. Dakota lifted off, his powerful wings flapping upwards. He landed on the windowsill, heat drifting outside from the open glass. He hopped in the room, panic starting to set in. Dakota heard Mr. Trent's voice outside the door, clearly on the phone with someone. He felt something warm and sticky lap over his talons, and Dakota's eyes fell to the floor. Callax was lying face down in a pool of his own blood, clothes soaked through.

Dakota held back a scream. This was worse than every nightmare he had ever had, every attacking word. He had been wished dead plenty of times, been to funerals, gotten the final letters in the mail. But this was different. This was too real. Trying to compose himself, he looked down at the wound, which didn't look so pretty.. Glancing back at the door to ensure it was still closed, Dakota tied his shirt tightly around the injury, hoping to slow the blood flow. He wanted to get help but was worried he wouldn't be able to make it back in time.

I need to get him out of here now! Dakota's mind screamed.

He hoisted Callax onto his shoulders, immediately collapsing under the weight. Callax was much bigger than him, and he was unconscious. Stumbling towards the window, he racked his brain for another solution. He had never tried flying when carrying more than his school bag, and if they fell from this height, he probably wouldn't make it. This felt like having his wings bound all over again, the thought of tumbling toward the ground… and taking Callax down with him. He clutched the windowsill, the height making him dizzy. He couldn't do it. He was just too scared. He would have to find some other way. He got ready to lower Callax onto the floor when he saw the door begin to open. He panicked, all the stories he had heard as a child pouring into the terror of this moment. He launched himself out the window, Callax over his shoulder. Dakota shut his eyes, clearing every thought but the hope that they could make it down.

Chapter Six

Willow Orio

Willow sat on the steps of the dark house, her shaking hands clenched tightly. She would give anything for Dakota and Callax to walk out of that awful place, smiling and telling her everything would be okay. She hated this feeling of helplessness, and that everyone could see her fear, all because of that wretched purple goo. But it wasn't like she was freaking out about nothing! That house was pure evil; she could feel it! Darkness and despair oozed from the walls like some vile disease, and just being near it made her feel like crying.

"Help!" Willow heard Dakota's shrill voice coming from the trees.

Panic sent another wave of sculk dripping off her face. She shot off into the thicket, wings scraping against sharp branches. Her brother was kneeling on the ground, wings looking like they had just hit every tree in his path. His shirt was tied around Callaxs chest, and Dakota seemed even smaller than usual next to Callaxs unconscious form. Blood and sculk was everywhere, which stained the green grass a reddish purple. Willow wanted to launch into the air and never come back down, to run away from all the problems she couldn't fix.

"Where's your shirt?" Tempest said snidely, clearly judging Dakota's small form.

Dakota hissed angrily, pulling Callax closer to him.

"What happened?" Pearl asked, her large emerald eyes glowing like fireflies in a swamp.

"I'll explain later," Dakota replied hastily, wings trembling. "Right now, I need help carrying him."

Pearl hoisted Callax's arm over her shoulder, stumbling under the pressure. Tempest glanced back at the road as if he was considering running back home before helping lift Callax to his feet.

"What now?" Tempest growled, his fangs glittering in the darkness.

"I can try to treat his wound, but I'm not sure how bad it is," Pearl said.

"Why don't we ask them for help?" Tempest asked, pointing upward. Mr. Trent was standing in the windowsill, three searchers staring over the edge.

Willow wanted to dig the most enormous hole in the world and sink into it forever. Dakota scrambled back, looking panicked.

"We have to leave now!" Dakota whispered sharply. "I'm almost positive they attacked Callax. He probably already called the Queen."

"Why would the searchers commit a crime?" Tempest puzzled, as if they had all day to answer stupid questions.

"They work for the queen! She probably ordered them to do it!" Dakota argued. "Look, we don't have time for this! Do you want to stay here and get captured?"

"The queen would never do that! She's a fair and just ruler. Besides, what's the motive? He's just some country kid." Tempest said righteously. "I'm sure if I just explain to the searchers this was all one big mistake, they'll let us all go home.

Her brother looked like he wanted to strangle someone.

"Don't you remember what she did to the Avians?" Dakota snapped. "She's the worst ruler of all time! She probably just enjoys killing people; no motive needed!"

Tempest ignored him, yelling up at the searchers, waving like he was trying to flag down a boat.

The searcher in the middle gave Tempest a long look before firing a shot right between him and Dakota.

Tempest dropped Callax, scrambling back as the bullet landed. His eyes widened, and he jumped to his feet.

"Stop!" Tempest yelled, hands cupped around his mouth as he tried to reach the figures on the balcony. "We're not with him! Stop shooting and we can clear up this misunderstanding."

The searchers didn't hear him, or just didn't care, because the bullets continued to rain down.

"Let's go!" Dakota yelled, grabbing Callax and getting ready to run. Pearl leaned over to support Callax's, his limbs completely limp on her shoulder. They started to limp off, going as fast as they could manage with an injured person. Willow followed behind, casting anxious glances back at Tempest. He was peering up at the window, still trying to convince the searchers they were on the same team.

"Willow!" Dakota chirped sharply. "Come on!"

"We can't go without him!" Willow insisted.

"Course you can!" Dakota hissed, dropping Callax and grabbing his sister's arm. Pearl stumbled, Callax crumpling onto her shoulder as Dakota's large wings slipped away.

"No!" Willow hissed, pulling out of her brother's grip and running beside Tempest. He turned to look at her, blue and brown eyes flashing in unison.

"Get out of here!" he snarled at Willow, backing away from the little Avian.

A bullet whizzed past his head, and Tempest pushed Willow away.

"I'm not with her!" He screamed, mouth wide like he had fishhooks stuck between his jaws. "Talk to me!"

Tempest looked up hopefully, before a shot nicked the side of his ear, leaving a semicircle of blood slowly dripping from his left side. He panicked, shooting beside the house after Willow and out of site from the searchers.

Pearl limped forward, spotting a large bush. The ground was hollowed out, leading under the house and to the foundation of the structure.

"In here." Pearl whispered, ducking behind the bush and into the crawlspace.

Dakota pulled Willow forward, pushing into the bush and folding his wings back to fit in the cramped space.

"Tempest!" Pearl said frantically, nearly out of breath. "Help me get Callax under."

Tempest didn't move, face frozen in disbelief as the blood from his ear began soaking into his silver hair.

"Please." Pearl asked, Callax starting to slip from her grip. "He's going to die if you don't help me."

Indisison warred on his face until he gave a short nod. He lifted Callax off of Pearl, easily getting both of them under the crawlspace, Pearl right behind him.

The space was terribly claustrophobic. Sediment was dripping from the ceiling like rain, the house above her feeling like a constant threat. Worms were wriggling around her hands, dirt tangling into her curtain-like hair. She looked over to Pearl, who was leaned over Callax pressing Dakota's grimy shirt against Callaxs chest. With her other hand she was brushing dirt off his face and neck, constantly fighting to keep his airway clear. Dakota was pulling a large shirt covered in dust over his small frame, clearly found beneath the house. It looked like it belonged to Mr. Trent judging on the size, and it could have been down there for years.

"I shouldn't have run." Tempest gasped pulling in on himself. "Oh no. no no NO!"

"Quiet!" Dakota hissed in Tempest's broken ear.

"It's not too late!" Tempest said loudly. "We can still go out and explain!"

"No." Dakota whispered. "Whether you like it or not, you're with us. What do you think happens when you come out of that foundation?"

"I just need to explain!" Tempest insisted.

"If you go out there they will shoot first, ask questions later! you were lucky they cant aim. Now that they're off the balcony, you're dead if you don't stop talking."

Tempest looked like he was about to snap back, but Dakota pressed his hand against his bloodied ear before pulling back, spreading his fingers to show Tempest the blood on his palm.

Willow heard the cocking of a gun, and Dakota pulled her farther back under the foundation of the house. Tempest snapped his mouth shut, suddenly aware of his situation. A mix of emotions were swirling around his head. Most of all fear, but not of being discovered. No, Tempest was afraid of being hidden. And he was afraid of the gun, which was the only thing keeping him quiet All Willow knew was that his fear isn't helping her own. She tried to focus on Pearl, the only one of them who wasn't either angry or terrified. Her friend was still hunched over Callax, aura radiating nothing but a wall. Pearl was like this anytime there was injury. She claimed it made it easier to tune out distractions.

Boots were showing through the bushes, clearly getting closer and closer to their hiding place. Dakota was shovling dirt against the wall, making the opening so small only he and Willow could fit through the entrance. Tempest immediately noticed this, and Dakota nearly had to smother him in order to keep him silent. Callax was flat on his back, breathing not even audible over the rustling of trees as the searchers tramped through the trees and around the house.

Pearl looked up slowly, blood dripping from her clenched hands. Willow didn't dare to even whisper, but she gave Pearl a pleading look and gestured to Callax, who had Dakota's dirty shirt over his white one. Pearl had zipped his blue jacket over top of the injury, using the thick fabric almost like a second layer of skin. Pearl shrugged, and Willow felt her chest start to flutter. She knew that gesture. Pearl was trying to make light of a situation. She only did that when she was unsure of the outcome.

"Sir, I dont think they're here." a young woman said, voice muffled by a visor. "Let's move to another area.

"Fine, one final check." the man replied.

Dakota relaxed his posture, but kept his hand cupped over Tempest's mouth. Willow felt relieved. As soon as the searchers were gone, they could take a breath and figure out what to do. Willow instantly stiffened, loud coughing filling the space. Callax was choking out a breath, his eyes half open like he was still under sleep.

"Sir, I heard something!" a searcher said excitedly, and Tempest mouthed something under his breath, a name Willow couldn't make out.

A sounding of boots rang in her ear, and she saw the searcher lean over and spot the bush. Dakota, in a moment of panic, shoved the final chunk of dirt into place, sealing up the entrance.

They were buried alive.

The searcher stared at the dirt for a long time, and Willow was doing everything not to breathe. Everyone was frozen, Except for Callax, who was practically deafening Willow with his noise. Pearl looked down, indecision clear on her face. Callax needed to shut up. He was going to get them caught if he kept that up, but it wasn't like they could stop him. They needed to keep his airway open. Dakota didn't realize, or he just didn't care, because he instantly released Tempest and shoved his hands over Callax's mouth. His chest heaved, sputtery coughing choking in his throat. Pearl looked panicked, but didnt pull Dakota's hands off. It was this or certain capture.

Willow pressed herself against the ground, silently praying that the searcher would leave. All she needed to do was move.

Please please please. Willow thought *Don't let us die like this. Don't let Callax suffocate because of us.*

A searcher sneezed loudly, and Willow heard an angry mutter. The boots stomped away, and Willow pulled back a small chunk of earth, letting air flood back into her lungs.

"Sir, it's just Felix." The woman scoffed, annoyed. "False alarm."

"They're not here." The older man said decisively. "Where do the others live?"

"Tempests a few houses down." The youngest replied.

"Good." the man muttered. "That's the next place they would have gone. Let's move out."

The searchers started off, and it was a good ten minutes before anybody said a word. The only noise was Callax raspy breaths and Tempest quiet anger. After Willow felt sure they were gone for good, she started to pull the rest of the dirt away from the entrance. She squeezed out from under the foundation, Dakota right behind her. Tempest dragged Callax out from under the house, his blue hoodie trailing against the ground. He pulled Callax upward, Dakota leaning over to help Pearl out. Tempest still looked shell shocked, and he was fiddling with the strings of Callaxs hoodie, who was over Tempest's shoulder.

"We can't stay here." Dakota said quietly, one wing folded over Willow's back.

Pearl nodded, and they started walking, the capitol behind them. Only Tempest looked back, frantic glances every few steps. Eventually, the castle was out of view completely, and all Willow could see was open fields dotted with ancient trees. Willow was fluttering above them, looking for a place to spend the night. She could see her brother beneath her, wings twitching unhappily. He clearly wanted to be up in the sky, but they had insisted he needed to help Tempest carry Callax. Tempest could have done it alone, but Dakota didn't trust him to do it properly. Willow spotted an outcropping of rock in the open plains, and it looked fine enough. They ducked inside, and Pearl set Callax down against the wall. She had started to weave long strands of grass together like bandages, and her hands moved like a spider making a web. Pearl was magic, Willow had no clue how her friend always seemed to work miracles. She had always been good with injury, and only now did Willow realize how useful that really was. Pearl had no formal training, but growing up in an active war zone taught fast. Willow was talking figuratively, but the only time she had been over to Pearl's house it might as well have been. She only stayed to grab a coat, but by that time she had already gotten hit twice, and somebody threw a ceramic bowl at them. Pearl tried to keep things casual, but Willow knew her friend had seen death.

"Well, the silver lining is that they're a terrible shot." Pearl smirked, her shoulders relaxing. "The bullet missed basically every important organ, so it could have been a lot worse.

"Does that mean he's gonna be okay?" Willow asked nervously.

"I wouldn't call getting shot okay exactly, it's definitely gonna hurt." Pearl replied, wiping the blood off her hands and onto the stone walls. "But he's gonna make it."

"I don't like this." Tempest said angrily. His shock had faded to frustration and rage the second they got out of sight of the castle, and Willow could almost see the gears in his head turning as he thought over the encounter.

"You don't like anything!" Dakota chirped snidely. "Nobody cares about your privileged opinions."

"I worked hard for my status!" Tempest cried indignantly. "But that's not the point. The Queen wouldn't order his execution unless he had done something! We could be sitting in a cave with a mass murderer for all we know. And nobody wants to ask any questions?"

"Get this through your thick head!" Dakota snapped. "The Queen would totally kill someone just for not being what she wants. Besides, if she sent away my family for looking different, I can believe she kills country kids just for kicks."

"You're impossible." Tempest snarled.

"The searchers attacked you." Dakota said righteously. "And you're not dangerous."

Willow felt her hands start to prick, panic fraying her nerves. Tempest was dangerous, and her brother was going to get himself killed if he wasn't careful. The former searcher could snap his neck without even trying, and Tempest had formal training. Dakota wouldn't win any fights with that boy, she was sure of it.

Tempest's reply was cut off by a smothered cough, and Willow saw Callax blink awake, his blue eyes glazed.

"You're up!" Dakota chirped happily, ignoring Tempest's angry barks.

"Ugggggg im- wh-what are we doing wh-where?" Callax muttered, voice groggy. "Owwwwww"

"Don't move yet." Pearl said quickly. "You have to give it time to seal."

"What?" He said, confusion muddled on his face. "Where's dad? He said he'd be here."

Willow felt her breath catch, all the emotion tearing at her heart. She could tell Callax was waiting, waiting for somebody he expected to be here. But the man he was picturing wouldn't ever come back, and everybody seemed to know that but him.

"It's alright." Pearl replied, letting her shoulders relax. "We're in the borderlands. Outside of the capitol."

Callax blinked hard, face twisted into an expression Willow couldn't decipher.

"They…" Callax started, clearly struggling with his words. "My familys gone, aren't they? And you, you go to my school?"

"Yep." Dakota said, sitting crisscross applesauce next to Callax. "You made me jump out a window. Thanks for that."

"Way to break it to him gently." Pearl rolled her eyes, face twisted into a smile.

"Um, sorry?" Callax replied, and Willow was unsure if he fully understood what he was apologizing for.

"All good." Dakota replied, leaning back on his wings. "So, what do you remember?"

"Uncle." Callax said. "He let somebody into my room, and, um"

Callax cut off, biting his bottom lip.

"Well, I guess we can start there." Dakota shrugged. "It was an eventful night anyway."

Willow didn't stay and listen to Dakota's dramatic retelling of the day's events. She was tired anyway, and her hands felt like they were being picked apart by crows. Trying to ignore the cracking of her skin, she curled her wings around her like a cocoon and floated off into dreams.

Chapter Seven

Tempest Rincher

Tempest believed he had a purpose. His entire life, he had strived for results. He wanted to make his family proud. He wanted to be the person he was supposed to be, to follow the logical plan he was supposed to follow. Sitting in this dry cave, he could imagine his parent's disappointed faces as he once again let others sabotage his future. What was he thinking! Following this chaotic group out into the woods! He should have turned himself in. He was told the Queen was just and fair. Once his parents told her who he would be someday, she would have to let him go.

But would my family want me back? That nagging voice in the back of his mind whispered. *After this? You're just a disappointment.*

He tried pushing that thought away, instead focusing on what he could see. It was night, bright stars sparkling across the sky. The constellations were clearer than in the city, calling him in with beautiful patterns. He looked down. He hated stars. Stupid wishes that never came true laughing at him from above. Besides, they looked like sculk, and he didn't like thinking about Avains unless it was to hate them. He glanced at Dakota, expecting him to be saying something sarcastic and annoying, but the little boy had already fallen asleep, his soft cooing filling the room like a lullaby.

"Funny to see him like that, hu?" Callax said, raspy voice grating Tempest's ears. He jumped, Callax words jarring him out of thought. Callax was sitting on his left side, and that ear was still damaged. It wasn't completely broken, but it felt awful. Searchers were supposed to have a keen hearing and sense of smell, and Tempest had always excelled at tracking. Now he felt like half of his world had been cut off, the steady stream of sound chopped right down the middle. Callax shouldn't have been able to startle him, yet another reason he was acting like a floppy walrus instead of a member of the most distinguished training program in the capitol.

"What?" Tempest snapped, annoyed at Callax for making Tempest think about his damaged hearing and his crumbling status.

"I said it's weird to see Dakota curled up like that." Callax repeated. "I mean, I haven't known him as long as you have, but from what I gathered I wouldn't expect him to sleep like a toddler."

"Tell me about it." Tempest snorted, unable to resist a chance to laugh about the little Avain. "I would have thought he didn't sleep at all."

"I wonder what he dreams about?" Callax said, tilting his head in mock curiosity.

"I bet he dreams about yelling at me." Tempest rolled his eyes, feeling a bit of his anger slip away.

"Did you just make a joke?" Callax teased, jabbing Tempest in the shoulder, before gritting his teeth.

"Ow." Callax muttered. "That was stupid. Pearl told me not to move."

"Well Pearl says a lot of things." Tempest snorted. "She's a bit of a pushover."

"I like this Tempest." Callax said, half laughing half coughing. "Who are you, and what have you done with my friend?"

Friend. His mind whispered. *Friend! What would Mother think of your new "friends?" that silly little fish, those forsaken Avians, and worst of all, him.* His eyes flicked to Callax. Tempest was so stupid. He never should have let his guard down. CALLAX was why he was sitting here with a bunch of ditzy nobodies, who would almost certainly take him down with them if he allowed it. He would not let this group of vagabonds steal his future from him. He had spent his whole life training to be a searcher, and he wasn't going to throw it away for anything. Callax could NEVER be his friend. How DARE Callax act like they could ever be friends after Callax ruined his life! Tempest didn't want to be the family disappointment. He was supposed to be carrying out a legacy, not sitting in a dank hole with two tweety birds, some fake comedian, and Mr. Tragic Backstory.

"Well, don't get used to it," Tempest growled darkly. "It was a one-time thing."

he shoved Callax away from himself, accidentally making contact with the wound. Tempest pushed back the guilt creeping into his thoughts as he stared at Callax. He was not about to feel bad about giving Callax a little push after everything he had done.

Callax looked at him for a moment, blue eyes flickering like a candle. Pearl let out a yawn and peeked over from her rock ledge.

"What happened?" She yelped, jumping down from her ledge. She looked dreadful, usually damp skin dry and flaky from dehydration. There was limited water here, and the hot plains clearly weren't good for her health.

"I-I just fell," Callax murmured, glancing back at Tempest with a look he couldn't decipher.

Why didn't he tell Pearl what really happened? What could he possibly gain by protecting my reputation?

It didn't matter. It was one of his twisted games. Rebels were smooth talkers, and Tempest would not let Callax drag him away from the truth. He had tricked him once, and that was enough.

"Can you go get some of the chamomile flowers outside?" Pearl asked, her usually bright green eyes almost gray. "I would, but..." she cut off, raising one arm with a helpless smile.

"Sure," Tempest replied with an edged tone. His father's words rang in his ears. Tempest wasn't stupid. He knew what was behind those flaming eyes. Callax was like a ticking time bomb, and if the Queen wanted him dead, who knew what he was capable of. In fact, he bet any one of these sociopaths would kill him if they got the chance. If Tempest wanted to fulfill his destiny, he would have to make a few...

sacrifices.

Chapter Eight

Pearl Ashi

"Here's the flowers," Tempest muttered, tossing a handful of crushed petals towards Pearl.

She stared down at the yellow shavings. These were far too crumpled to work, but she wasn't about to tell Captain Overreaction that. It was just like at home—smile inside and out. She had been upset enough times about real problems to let a few smothered flowers bother her.

"Thanks." She said, grinning wryly. "Even if they look like they've been put through a garbage disposal."

"Whatever," he stalked away and curled up to sleep.

"I'll be okay," Callax said; his breathing had steadied, flaming eyes back to quiet embers. "He did his best."

"So," Callax inquired. "What do you think your family will do when they find out you're missing?"

She snorted, humored by the idea of her family even noticing she was gone. "They don't care. They've been adopting kids for years, they would be quite pleased if one disappeared."

"You're adopted?" Callax said sympathetically.

"Yep," she replied nonchalantly. "It's nothing like your situation, so don't feel bad. I never knew my parents, and according to the public records, my mom was single and simply didn't want a kid. She dropped me off at the orphanage, and only a few years later, I was picked up by some couple. They don't care about me, or any of us. Only their precious baby boy, who basically drove me out of the house."

"Oh, I'm so sorry." He replied, placing his hand over hers. Pearl felt her heart jump, and she suddenly hated the thought that he was going to let go of her hand.

"It's all good." she smiled.

'Why would they adopt kids they don't care about?" Callax asked, his tail sending small flames across the cavern.

"The free support money the queen gives them for taking the little gremlins off her hands," Pearl said, shrugging her shoulders. "Most of us don't actually live at home. Usually, I sleep at the bottom of the lake."

"This is actually a great opportunity to get away from my parents," she remarked. "If it wasn't so hot, I could count this as a vacation."

Callax rolled his eyes, but Pearl could see the smile he was hiding. It made her heart flutter, seeing his bright blue eyes. She knew it was stupid, but she couldn't help it. His face was just so…

"Hey, I've been meaning to ask," Callax started, jarring her out of her thoughts. "Where did you learn to deal with bullet wounds? I assumed your mom was a nurse or something, but I'm guessing she wouldn't be the best teacher."

"Um, I kinda just picked it up," she replied, tightening her grip on his hand. "One day, some kid at home, one of the older boys I think, well, he was messing with a gun in the house. I think he got it from a friend. Anyway, he caught my left shoulder, and I panicked. I just shoved some toilet paper on it to stop the bleeding. I was 9, pretty sure. This sort of thing is really common at my house, and my parents don't think it's worth the medical cost to fix it. So, I kept sneaking over to the university to look through the class windows. I infected a few cuts, but I'm much better now. It saved me a lot of pain, too; nobody wants to attack the one kid who can keep them from dying."

"You've seen people die? Like in front of you?" Callax asked, face pale.

"Yeah, seen a few," Pearl said casually. "The kids are usually replaced by next week. I've saved some people, but I'm definitely not perfect. It would be better if they had something real."

"Look, I," Callax stuttered as if he was searching for words. "I mean, thank you. You saved my life; I just thank you."

She nodded briefly, ducking away to hide her blushing face. She could see the scorched grass coating rolling hills out the cave door. Believe it or not, she was excited to finally leave the capitol, to travel the world, and if she was lucky, maybe things would change. She knew thinking like that was wrong, but she couldn't help but feel that if the system was perfect, the Avians would still be around, and, well, her home would be a bit better. She didn't care about politics, and she didn't mind the gaping holes in the Queen's logic. She was more of a go-with-the-flow kind of person. What did annoy her was that whenever she had a question, no one would give her an honest answer. After a while, she realized no one ever would, and that it was easier to just pretend everything was one big joke. If life was never meaningful, death didn't matter. It still hurt; how could it not, but it was easier to push through. No matter what happened, she could laugh about it tomorrow.

Chapter Nine

Dakota Orio

"Rise and shine!" Dakota chirped loudly, accidentally smacking Tempest with his flaring wings.

"Can you keep your creepy space goo on your side of the cave," Tempest muttered, turning over like he wanted to go back to sleep.

"No can do," Dakota replied, grinning as he purposely dripped sculk over Tempest's arbitrary line. "Besides, we have to leave the cave today; who cares if it gets a little dirty?"

"Were leaving?" Willow echoed, looking up from her sleeve. It was covered in beautiful paintings of birds and flowers, so realistic you could have mistaken them for the real thing. She had transformed the cold stone floor around her into a haven of color, with gorgeous spiral patterns snaking across the decrepit cave. Dakota could tell she was disappointed about leaving all her hard work behind, and he thought it was a shame something so wonderful was stuck on the grimy floors.

"Sorry." Dakota warbled, tucking in his wings so he wouldn't get any sculk on her painting. "But if Tempests right, we have to be out of here and on the move by sundown."

"Right about what?" Tempest growled, turning his angry glare towards Dakota and Willow.

"That we have to leave soon," Willow replied gently, as if she was worried that her voice alone would make Tempest mad.

"You listened to my advice?" Tempest asked, looking offended that Dakota wasn't fitting his stereotype.

"Pearl listened." Dakota snorted. "Which is fair. The former searcher would know more about tracking anyway. Besides, Callax can walk fine right now, and we should move while we can."

"Willow?" Pearl asked, gesturing towards the explosion of color coating the hard stone. "Did you paint this? It's soooo pretty." She was grinning, no surprise there, but it filled Dakota with triumph to see people admire his sister's hard work. Willow smiled shyly, and Dakota even noticed a few dots of sculk on her hand before she wiped it away. Dakota wished she could just be proud of herself without pushing it away. He remembered when she was little, she used the celestial liquid like paint. She would sit in her room for hours, using her clever fingers to spread the ooze into beautiful constellations. Those paintings were always his favorites, and he thought it was a real shame that she'd thrown them all away after the banishment.

Tempest stalked over to Willow, his tail sending dust cascading over her painting. He lifted her into the air by the sleeve of her sweater and shoved her into the wall.

"WHAT WERE YOU THINKING!" Tempest roared, his sharp canine teeth glinting like miniature daggers. "DO

YOU WANT THE SEARCHERS TO KNOW WE WERE HERE?"

Blood roared in Dakota's ears, drowning out any coherent thoughts he could have had. He lunged forward, slamming into Tempest with all his force. He tumbled backward, sending a stalactite buried in the cave wall crashing down. It shattered like glass, and Dakota felt a torrent of little rocks pricking into his wings. He let out a furious chirp, easily being thrown off by the more muscular boy. He was slammed into the ground, and Dakota could feel his breath escaping as Tempest added more and more pressure onto his throat. He could hear Willow squawking in the background, begging him to stop. Dakota stared into his multi-colored eyes, expecting something completely feral, but he looked really calm. Not gloating, not mad, just determined. Tempest looked like he knew exactly what he was doing, and for some reason, he seemed to think it was necessary. Dakota glared at him, trying to put all his pent-up rage into the most furious expression he could muster. He would die again and again to protect his flockmates, and he wanted Tempest to feel as bad as possible about it. Someone suddenly pulled the weight off Dakota's chest, and he bolted upright, preparing to rush back into the fight. Tempest was kneeling next to Callax, his raspy breathing filling the cave like toxic gas. Tempest looked like he'd seen a ghost, pressing himself against the wall. A long piece of shiny metal was on the floor, and Callax kept trying to push himself upwards to no avail. Dakota could have sworn that his left leg was just… gone. But that was impossible. He didn't even look hurt!

"Wh-what?" Tempest stuttered, glancing at the silver object.

"U-hh," Callax muttered, clearly uncomfortable with the suspicion in Tempest's voice. "Can you pass me that?" He pointed at the strange metal contraption.

Pearl stared at him for a moment before handing him the device. Callax took one last look at Tempest before snapping the item into place right below his knee.

Oh, du! The weird wrinkles in his jeans, the way his left shoe never fit, it was so obvious!

Tempest, on the other hand, didn't seem to get the message.

"Y-you!" Tempest shrieked, backing away. "I knew it! You're some kind of rebel bomb here to destroy us all! You want me dead!"

"I promise I'm not a bomb!" Callax replied hastily, standing up with his hands raised non-threateningly. "It's just a prosthetic, not a big deal."

"How does it work?" Pearl asked, curiosity sparkling in her light green eyes.

"Is that really your most pressing question?" Tempest hissed, somehow still not convinced Callax wasn't a robot.

"Please stop fighting." Willow pleaded, a trickle of blood flowing from where her head hit the rocks. Even in her delirious state, she wasn't letting any sculk creep onto her face. "I'm sorry."

Dakota couldn't believe she actually thought this was her fault. Tempest had just attacked her, and Willow was blaming herself. He wished he could show her how incredible she was and that she would never deserve to be treated that way. Not by Tempest, not by the Headmaster, not by anyone.

"Well, we should head out. I don't feel like getting beheaded today, no thank you." Pearl chuckled nervously.

Dakota nodded, excitement setting his mind alight. He could feel his feathers twitching, sculk seeping from his eyes and over his wings. Despite the situation, he couldn't wait to fly across the open sky with no one to tell him he was useless or that he would never amount to anything. Out there, away from the billboards and angry teachers, he would be truly free for the first time in his life. And once you let a bird out of its cage, it won't ever return.

Chapter Ten

Mr. Trent

Mr. Trent hadn't always been a slave to his own fear. He remembered playing with his brother, pretending they were brave knights, standing up for what was right. But now his brother was dead, and it was all because he was a coward who gave up his humanity to save his own skin. His Nephew Callax was probably bleeding out somewhere in the wilderness because he was terrified of saying no. An entire race was taken from their homes because he was too scared not to follow orders. And now he was alone. No friends, no family, and willing to do anything to stay alive. Prepared to give in to his fear and regret it forever.

"Come in," the Queen hissed from behind the grand doors. Mr. Trent stepped inside, dread turning his bones to ice. A soft candle illuminated the dark room, sending long shadows dancing across the wooden floors. Headmaster Onix stood behind the Queen, her black hair straightened perfectly down her back.

"Oh, look." Queen Indigo spat, smoke rising from her mouth like poison. "It is everyone's favorite failure."

This is it. He thought sadly. *I'm going to die, and all of the awful things I've done will be for nothing.*

"I'm sorry, Your Majesty," he whispered, bowing deeply. "I wish only to serve you."

"Stop with the self-pitying nonsense," the Queen barked sharply, her tail smacking into her ankles. I didn't summon you to hear your pathetic excuses."

"Why did you summon him?" the Headmaster asked, claws digging into the wooden desk. "All he does is stand around."

"Yes, but he must know something about his little rebel of a nephew." the Queen replied, staring at him like he was a fun new toy that she couldn't wait to mess with.

"I never met him," Mr. Trent whispered, suddenly thinking of his older brother. He had gotten a letter nearly fifteen years ago inviting him to meet his nephew. That was the last family function he was asked to attend. Not that he ever came, but it hurt to know he was cut off. He chose this.

"His band of friends?" The Queen pressed. "Know anything about them?"

"I do." Headmaster Onix interjected, more fury in her voice than Mr. Trent would have thought was possible. "According to the searchers, two of the little rats are Avians. The male is particularly evil. He was a rebel just waiting to happen."

"What about the female?" Queen Indigo asked.

"She's naive to almost a comical degree. She'd put her life in danger to help a slug. But the male seems to be fiercely protective of her. Probably some bird-brained Avian instinct."

the Headmaster growled, hate burning in her black eyes. "All of them are stupid, actually. I bet if we captured one, the rest would march up to the palace in a foolish display of chivalry. All they want is to feel like little heroes."

"What are you proposing?" Queen Indigo inquired, her matt black robes falling over her chair in perfect waves.

"We just need to capture one of them." The Headmaster smiled, her pearly white teeth glinting in the candlelight. "It doesn't matter which one. The rest will come."

The Queen paused for a moment as if contemplating the idea. "Good plan. Trent, organize the troops." she commanded. "I want you to be the head of this operation. It's your mess."

This is your chance. He thought. *Be brave. Stand up to her. Change for the better. Break free.*

No

He pushed the idea of rebellion out of his mind once again. He'd picked his side the moment he watched the bombs go off in silence, and it was far too late to go back. He would always regret his actions, but if he turned back now and died a martyr, it would have all been a waste. The truth of the matter was that he was alive, and he was willing to do anything to keep it that way.

Chapter Eleven

Willow Orio

.Willow could feel the breeze winding around her wings like a wispy ribbon. The air was clearer out here than it had ever been in the city, lifting her higher and higher into the blue sky. She could have stayed up there every day of her life, no fighting, no one to call her fragile or too soft. Sculk covered her wings, slowly pouring over her face until constellations were all she could see. It was magical, letting her emotions run free, unworried about what others would think. She didn't care when she was younger, but things were different now. The last thing she wanted was people whispering about her, wondering what caused the steady drip of visible feelings. That's why she'd repainted everything in her room. It was awful to see the dark stains coating the beautiful objects, knowing she had ruined them forever. But in the endless clouds, there was nothing to wreck.

"It's great up here, isn't it?" Dakota chirped, fluttering beside her.

Willow squawked in surprise, almost falling out of the sky in her panic. She frantically wiped her face with the inside of her sweater, embarrassed that her brother had seen her like this. The fabric was a midnight blue with starry patterns, evidence of the many times she'd used the garment to remove sculk. Most of her clothes were like this, pristine on the outside, ragged on the inside. It was better to keep it all tucked away, where the only one it damaged was her.

"Y-yeah," she stuttered, face still buried in her sleeve.

"You do know you're allowed to be happy, right?" Dakota teased, pushing Willow's hair out of her face, leaving the strands a tangled mess of sculk.

"I know!' Willow replied indignantly, pushing his hand away and sweeping her long hair back into place.

"Are you mad at the sculk or me?" he asked, only half joking. "I just want to make sure you're okay."

Annoyance pricked at Willow like barbed wire tearing at her from the inside. He didn't understand. He loved trailing sculk on things, able to think of it as leaving his mark instead of feeling endlessly guilty about destroying something someone worked hard on. He would tear the world down if he thought it would bring the right person to justice, never taking her seriously when she told him she could handle something on her own. She was just his shy little sister; that was all she'd ever be. They were a flock, which meant always looking out for each other, but since the deportation of the Avains, he was getting to be almost too pushy. She missed when they could hang out without Dakota getting all hot and bothered over her problems.

Dakota stared at her for a long moment, worry flickering in his purple eyes. Willow felt guilt clawing at her stomach at seeing her brother's distress. She knew he loved her, and it was truly painful to see him upset. She squeezed his hand reassuringly, relief flooding over her as her brother's face relaxed.

"I'm perfectly fine." she soothed, steading her breathing to clear away the rest of the sculk.

"I came up to get you for lunch." He replied casualty, wings beating like mini helicopters. "Callax was unfolding a picnic blanket when I left."

Where in the world did you get a picnic blanket?" Willow asked.

"Ok-ay." Dakota huffed, "You got me. Tempest fell asleep, and I might have cut his jacket into scrap fabric."

"DAKOTA." Willow chirped hotly. "You don't need to get into any more trouble."

"It's too warm to use the coat anyway," he said, waving her concerns off. "Besides, I needed to get a little revenge for how he treated you earlier."

Willow felt anxiety jab at her chest like a stalactite. Nothing good would come of this; she could feel it. She'd seen the look in Tempest's multi-colored eyes when he looked at them. She was sure her brother would have been dead if Callax had not stepped in, and it would have been her fault.

"Race ya!" Dakota yelled, shooting down through the clouds like a falcon.

Willow rolled her eyes before darting after her older brother.

~

The cave was a mess, food and sculk all over the floor. Tempest was facedown in the sun, looking angry even in sleep. He was wearing a black tank top, his jacket laid out in pieces across the cold stone.

"Your back," Callax said, waving cheerfully at Willow.

"Hi," she murmured, sensing the pain deep in his chest. She could feel the air thickening near the wound, and she was shocked no one had noticed yet. "Where's Pearl?"

"Right here!" Pearl chucked, holding up an armful of wheat stalks. "Making food for the rest of you lazy weirdos!"

Pearl was clearly disheveled, green eyes faded to a swampy gray. Her usually tan skin was the color of old chlorine, and her smile looked almost forced. If Willow didn't know better, she wouldn't have thought this was Pearl at all.

"Do you need some help?" Willow asked, trying to keep her tone casual.

"Na," Pearl replied. "It's fine. Besides, your brother was supposed to be the one helping me."

"Sorry, I got a bit distracted," Dakota mumbled, not looking sorry in the slightest.

Suddenly, Willow felt like she could fall through the floor at any moment. Sharp needles stabbed at her talons like claws, and the world suddenly tilted on its head. Her wings were trembling, and she could sense the vibrations in the air. Every shift in the breeze, the dust on the ground, the thick swamp of emotions swirling around her… she could feel all of it.

"Are you alright?" Dakota asked. "You zoned out for a moment.

"Fine," she responded, ensuring she could still breathe. This had happened before, at the Trent house, when she was about to start school, the night of the deportation. Something terrible was going to happen; she was sure of that. She couldn't tell how she always seemed to know, but she hadn't been wrong yet.

Chapter Twelve

Callax Trent

"Callax! Wake up!"

Callax could feel someone kicking him awake, the sharp end of the boot driving into his side. It was probably Tempest, as he was sure the others would be more careful. But he doubted that Tempest cared about accidentally breaking his ribs.

"I'm coming, I'm coming." He muttered, sitting up to see his friends standing beside a woman in her early twenties. She was wearing a hijab in a dusty purple color, and her eyes looked almost identical to Willows in shape. The stars were reflecting off her dress, making her look as if she was made of constellations. And she was staring at him like the universe depended on it.

"Who the hell are you?" Callax asked, more shocked than scared.

The strange woman dipped into a slight bow. "I'm Nevia," she said. "I fled from the palace to find you. Your effect on the future is bigger than many before it. I believe the Queen has grown callous and cruel, and freedom can only be achieved with her removal. And the universe has informed me that you are the key to that freedom."

Dakota leapt forward, perching on Nevia's shoulders like he had known her for years. He looked ecstatic, excitement radiating from his crooked grin.

"This is the Queen's top seer." Dakota chirped, voice high with pleasure. "She said you're destined to kill the Queen!"

"WAIT, WHAT!" Tempest cried, his bored expression shifting to panic. "No one told me about this! Why would that be the key to anything?"

"Are you kidding me!" Dakota squawked, regarding Tempest with a dumbfounded look. "This is wonderful news! The Avians will finally be free!"

Kill the Queen… Callax ran the words over in his mind. *Is that what I'm meant to do? Could I really kill someone? Do I want to?*

"I was right," Tempest whispered, his voice raising after every word. "He's just another filthy rebel."

"That's a good thing!" Dakota shot back. "Your mighty ruler has been harassing my family for over 8 years! She deserves to die!"

"Both of you stop!" Callax yelled, jumping in between the shouting pair. "I don't know what I'm going to do, but it's going to be my choice. I don't want anyone else to decide my future."

Nevia looked at him with pity in her eyes. "I wish it could be so, but your fate has already been foretold. The stars themselves have chosen you. You must accept that."

"See?" Tempest gloated, his razor-sharp canines glinting like silver. "He's a killer at heart. How long before he goes after the Queen's workers, like, oh, I don't know, the searchers?"

"Stop being horrible!" Willow cried, grabbing Tempest's hand like she was trying to soften his anger. "You can't possibly think Callax would hurt you?"

Tempest yanked his hand away, looking disgusted at the contact. "I doubt that revenge can be drowned out by one death. How many monsters stopped their rampage after seeing the first body?"

"We would only do what was necessary for justice," Dakota muttered.

"Tell me, little bird, how far would you go?" Tempest challenged, his eyes reflecting years of hatred. "Would you kill a searcher with your own hands to free your precious flock? Would you kill me? How about the rest of us? Does someone willing to do that really deserve to be free? Don't you think there's a reason the Avians were sent away? I know the truth. You're all little monsters."

Dakota lunged forward, his wings flaring. The pair fell to the ground, hissing and screeching. Blood and sculk flew across the clearing, seeping into Dakota's borrowed shirt. Willow pulled on her brother's wings, her panicked chirping filling the room with a frantic aura. Pearl had somehow slept through all of this, her chest rising and falling with rapid breaths.

"Stop!" Nevia yelled, her voice even-tempered. "I didn't walk all this way to watch the children of the prophecy tear each other apart."

To his surprise, Dakota was the first to back away. He looked… guilty, like a child who had broken his mother's dishes.

He must really believe this lady can help him. Callax thought, feeling even more expectations piled onto his shoulders. He didn't want all of Dakota's dreams to be dependent on him. The Avian would make a much better hero, anyway.

"So I just have to accept this? Let the rest of you drag me down?" Tempest growled, spitting out a long white feather that had gotten stuck between his teeth. "You want me to just let you ruin our orderly society? Do you know how hard I worked for my searcher's license? Why should I throw away my dreams for a handful of birds?"

Willow folded in her wings, not a single drop of sculk on their pristine surface. It surprised him, considering that she had been screaming just a second ago, but Willow was remarkably good at staying in control.

"You can make new dreams," she cooed, her hand resting softly on his shoulder. Whoever becomes the new ruler will have a royal guard. You could be happy."

Tempest's eyes flickered briefly as if he was considering Willows's advice before they returned to their stony glare. He smacked her hand away, and his mussels were stiffing into iron.

"Maybe the rest of you could be happy being average, but I can't accept that. Everything was perfect. Until you came along." Tempest snarled, locking his gaze on Callax. "You could have just stayed away, and we would all be safe at home. Do you really think those bombs were a coincidence? Have you ever realized your family died because of you? The entire world would be better off if you were never here."

Callax felt like he was dissolving. Tempest couldn't have picked words that had hurt him more. Hundreds of people. A whole community. All dead.

Was it his fault?

Willow let out a small gasp and crumpled to the ground. Her wings covered her back like a blanket, and she was wringing her hands together tightly.

"Get down!" she hissed, a tiny bit of sculk pouring over her left wing. "They're here!"

"Who?" Dakota asked, crouching down beside her. He ran his fingers over her wings, trying to calm her down.

"The searchers," she murmured, her voice almost unintelligible from the wind outside. "They finally found us."

Chapter Thirteen

Tempest Richter

The searchers. Tempest thought, excitement rushing over him like a tidal wave. *They came back for me! This nightmare was finally going to be over! I can make up for all my mistakes!*

Dakota was already pressing himself into the ground, whispering reassurance into Willow's ear. Pearl was sleeping on the rock ledge behind him, the little dope. Callax was fumbling with his prosthetic as if he wasn't sure how to bend far enough. Nevia was just staring at him, her starry eyes seeming to look right through him. If he didn't know any better, he would have assumed she could read his mind. Her mouth never moved, but Tempest could have sworn he heard whispering in his ear, softly murmuring his doubts. He let out a slight hiss and tried to push his fears away. He knew this was the right thing to do. He would finally be everything his parents expected of him, a future searcher. There was no way he would throw away his chance.

He turned away from Nevia's judgemental eyes and ran to the center of the clearing without a second thought. At this point, the helicopter's whirring blades were deafening, and clumps of earth hit his skin like tiny meteors. Breathing was proving to be a chore, gas from the helicopter filling his lungs like some sort of vapor.

"Hey!" Tempest yelled, pointing toward the campsite. "The rebels are down there!"

Tempest squinted at the vehicle, confused as to why they hadn't sent a squadron down to meet him yet.

"CAN YOU HEAR ME?" Tempest cried, his voice rising in panic.

What if they don't want me? Tempest thought, urgency building in his chest. He refused to spend another day in this nightmare of an existence. He needed his life back. Now.

Just as he was about to try to jump up at the helicopter, his head slammed into the dirt. He could feel a mass of feathers pressing him to the ground, angry chirping, smothering him like weeds in a garden. Tempest was desperately reaching for air, but wings were folding around him, slashing claws dragging closer and closer to failure.

"You sick monster!" Dakota hissed, hands tightening around Tempest's throat. "You're going to get Willow killed!"

Tempest could hear blood roaring in his ears, sculk dripping off Dakota's clenched hands and onto the dry grass.

"That little bird doesn't know what she got into," Tempest muttered, his words barely coherent over the whirring helicopter. "The rebels always die in the end."

Dakota let out a roar of fury and pressed his beating wings harder against the dirt.

Tempest turned his eyes to the sky. Tangles of netted rope were falling over the fighting pair, dividing the sky into uneven sections. Dakota barely noticed, the Avian seemingly tuning out the rest of the world. Tempest felt his self-righteous anger burning a hole in his mind, satisfied that the Avian rebel would finally get what was coming to him. As for Tempest, he was finally going home.

~

"Get up."

Tempest could hear his mother's cold voice echoing in his ear. He sat up, careful to make sure he was standing straight. He was in a dark cell, the cold stone floor hard against his bare paws. There was only a single candle, illuminating a set of iron shackles on the back wall. It wasn't exactly how he had imagined his glorious homecoming, but he never expected all his fantasies to be accurate. Mother had always liked gray, after all.

"You better have an explanation for this." His mother murmured, her stony face cracking into a bittersweet smile. Her ears were twitching, eyes flicking to the security cameras behind them. She rested her clammy hand on his shoulder, a rare act of affection. His family wasn't the lovey-dovey type, and Tempest couldn't remember the last time his mother touched him outside of training.

"The Queen's waiting for you upstairs," his mother said gruffly. "Said she needed to ask you a few questions."

"Will you be joining us?" Tempest asked, unwilling to relax his pose until he was home. After all, the palace was a work setting, and he wanted to show his mother he could act like a professional.

She took a deep breath and pulled her hand away. "I can't. The Queen requested a private meeting. Besides, I will be gone on a search all week. I trust that you will act as you've been taught. Now get up there and make your family proud."

Tempest walked up the creaking stairs, disappointed that his parents couldn't come with him. Not that he was surprised. He never even saw them most days, and their long missions caused them to spend most nights away from home. They cared a lot about their work, and Tempest had gotten used to doing things alone.

He turned the handle on the audience chamber door, but it was yanked open from the other side and he fell forward. The room was bright. Too bright. The Queen was sitting on her throne, crown gleaming with emeralds and onyx. Mr. Trent, who Tempest had met during searchers training, was standing beside the Queen. His blue eyes were dull and guarded, the older man looking straight into Tempest's eyes like a fly caught in a web.

"Your majesty!" Tempest cried, falling into a deep bow.

"Don't pretend you're on our side, rebel." she hissed, twirling her claws around her necklace.

"Wha-what?" Tempest stuttered, wondering if he had missed something. Two searchers stepped into the room, standing in front of the door.

"Our squadron spotted you assisting a group of known criminals fleeing the city." the Queen growled, her tail flicking gemstones off the side of her throne. "If you think you're going to weasel your way back into our training program, you're wrong."

"I wasn't helping them!" Tempest stepped back, his voice rising. "I swear!"

"Save your breath. All that matters is you're the perfect bait. And after that, your execution will make the perfect example for other little traitors." the Queen growled, her eyes narrowing to paper-thin slits. "It's nothing personal, I thought you could have made an excellent searcher one day. A real shame."

"No," Tempest murmured, tears clouding his vision. "You're making a mistake, I'm still a searcher."

"Not anymore." the Queen said plainly.

Tempest stood there for what seemed like an eternity, feeling his world crumble around him. He glanced at the guards behind him, recognizing more and more of his friends. The kids who he grew up with, the people who would stay over during search nights so he wouldn't be alone. The people that could have been his siblings.

Isn't anyone going to tell her she's wrong? Tempest thought, hoping one of his friends would even acknowledge they knew him. He was blinking rapidly, trying to wake up from a dream that wasn't there. Suddenly, the hilt of a gun slammed into his head, and the world went black.

Chapter Fourteen

Pearl Ashi

Pearl woke up to the sound of pain. She could hear Willows shrieking, hot tears streaming down her sculk-covered face. Callax was pinning Willow to the ground, the only thing preventing the Avian from darting off into the sky. Pearl looked around the room for the others but couldn't see them. In fact, she couldn't see much at all. Most of the world was foggy at this point, fiery oranges and reds dancing across her vision. Every few seconds, she could spot a young woman through the sunset, but her features were a tangled mess.

"Silence!" the newcomer shouted, her voice forceful and calm simultaneously. Callax was responding to the lady whose name sounded like Nevia, but Pearl couldn't be sure over the fire in her ears.

Willow blinked at her, face raw with emotion. Pearl had never seen her friend so expressive; the usual mask of calm shattered into pure anger and despair. Willow was still being held back by Callax, but her wings were starting to fold back into submission.

"Listen to me," Nevia said, leaning down to face Willow. "Your brother is one of the most resilient, fearless people I have ever met. I know he will survive."

Willow fumbled with her sleeve, rubbing it against her face and smearing sculk around the edges. She looked up at Nevia, brown eyes almost purple in the dim light.

"Was that a prophecy?" Willow asked, her quiet chirping muffled by sobs.

Nevia shook her head. "That's just faith," she reassured, running her fingers through Willow's tangled hair. "I need you to stay strong for me. For everyone. We still need you."

Willow nodded, and Callax released her wings, settling beside the young Avain.

Pearl wanted to wrap her friend in a hug, joking and laughing with her until all their problems faded away. She would do it without hesitation but wasn't sure she could stand up without passing out.

"What are we going to do?" Callax murmured, his blue eyes flickering like a dying candle. "We can't just leave them there."

"We won't," Nevia said, voice firm. "But we shouldn't just charge into the palace without a plan. I say we rest here for a while, and then we can sneak in to get the others."

"He was all I had left," Willow murmured, her expression glazed over. "What will my flock be if he never comes home?"

Callax pulled Willow into a hug, her silver tears soaking into his jacket. She looked so fragile in his powerful arms, feathery wings limp against the ground.

Pearl eased herself down the ledge, praying she wouldn't fall off. She didn't know why it was suddenly so hard to climb, but it probably had something to do with the dust in her eyes. She stumbled forward, wincing as the ripped fin on her tail hit the ground, throwing off her already unsteady balance. She sank to the ground, her friend's dirty wings curving around her as she struggled to look through the fire.

"You're awake." Callax smiled weakly, and Pearl noticed his white shirt was an alarming red color.

"Are you okay?" Pearl asked, unsure if the blaze in her lungs was playing tricks on her again. "Your shirt is dirty."

He glanced down, smile fading into a grimace. "I think it's bleeding again. Sorry to cause more trouble, but do you think you can re-bandage it real quick."

"Yeah-yeah," she replied, alarmed at how creaky her voice sounded. "I can fix that. Do you have another piece of fabric I can use?"

"We can use Tempest's hoodie scraps," Callax said, and Willow sobbed, her warbles reminding Pearl of a wounded dove.

Pearl nodded, fumbling for the cloth. She tied it around Callax's chest, the starry color fading to a deep red. Her hands were shaking, dust compressing her lungs until she could barely breathe. His skin was so warm, the contact sending her heart into nervous flutters. She pushed it away, scolding herself for thinking like that right now.

"You look tired," Callax murmured, his speech jumbled in roaring flames. "Do you need something?"

Water! Pearl's mind rasped, even her thoughts seemingly coated in dust. More than anything, Pearl wanted water. The lake, a stream, even just a little rain. She could feel the edges of the world slipping away as more and more of her sight was covered in the blaze. She wouldn't even be surprised if she died tonight. That would be disappointing. She wanted to make a lot more puns before she died. She could tell Callax, ask to keep going, try to find a river before it was too late. She wanted to, she really did. But Callax was hurt, and Willow was crying, and the last thing they should be doing was galavanting across the open plains. Pearl had read enough books to know her role in this daring rescue. She was the comic relief. The cheerleader. She was the person who stood behind the real heroes. If she broke down now, all she would be was dead weight. She would be useless in a sword fight or a battle of wits. She would never be able to stop the problems. She needed to use what she was good at. She needed to keep smiling, keep laughing, and make sure that her friends never gave up. After all, what's a little fire when the world is burning down around you?

She grinned, forcing her green eyes to match her shining smile.

"Nothing at all!" she replied, her voice as chipper as she could manage. I've never been better. Now, who's ready to go change the world?"

"Kill a queen, save a brother, and manage to get Tempest to stop yelling?" he said sarcastically. "That might be a bit too much."

Callax lifted his eyes to look at Pearl, brushing her matted hair out of her eyes. Her heart felt like it would explode, his warm hand lingering on her cheek like a sunbeam. Eventually, he pulled his hand back, turning his blue eyes to face the ground.

Pearl let her mind drift away, worries flickering through her head. She didn't know if her parents would even care if she never came back. Would her little brother wonder where his playmate had gone? Would the people she had saved have a little funeral? Would her bullies miss tormenting her? Would her friends forget she was ever here? Did it even matter? The world would just keep spinning, and life would go on with or without her. Years from now, her name would be barely a whisper in someone's memory, and then she would be gone. Forgotten. But that was okay. She was finally uncovering the answers to the questions she had been asking forever. She was seeing the world! It was worth it to be part of the new future, at least for a little while. Her role was almost done. All that was left was to watch the fire burn on, hoping the flames of change wouldn't leave her behind in the blaze.

Chapter Fifteen

Dakota Orio

"Come on!" Dakota growled, slamming his weight into the barred door. "Work!"

He stumbled back, the force of the impact dislodging another feather from his battered wings. They hung limply at his side, so torn that he could hardly lift them. Dakota could see through the rough membrane of his feathers, and he wasn't even sure he could still fly. He might never fly again. Helicopter blades were sharper than he thought, but it was worth a shot. Any chance of escape would be worth it, no matter the cost.

Besides, it wasn't like he had anywhere to fly to. The room was terribly claustrophobic, with thick iron walls closing in on themselves like a dome. The ceiling was close enough to touch it with his arm extended. There wasn't even a crack in the wall for light to seep through. It was, overall, the most miserable place he had ever been. And if he overheard correctly, it might be the last.

"Worth it," he muttered. "They'll know I'm right."

Dakota wasn't quite sure why he kept talking to himself. Maybe it was just nice to hear a voice in the darkness. But it felt good. Good to pretend he still had his flock and wasn't all alone in the inky black. It was like his own little rebellion. A way to show the Queen he wouldn't play the games on her terms. Willow was safe right now, and that meant he had already won.

He could hear footsteps and large paws scraping against the dungeon floor. The conversation was almost silent, but he could still make it out.

"Why don't we just knock it out?" the quiet voice hissed from outside the iron door.

"You heard Her Majesty." a woman growled, her voice muffled like she was wearing a mask. "The drug is too strong for that thing. Just a teaspoon of the stuff, and it would never wake up."

"Be careful, Mirage. It probably has rabies or some other horrible disease."

WHAT! Dakota thought indignantly. *I'm NOT it! I'm a person! Just like them! And I do NOT have rabies!*

Another wave of fury washed over him, sculk flowing into his eyes, masking any rational thoughts he had left. Dakota wanted to scream, to taunt them until they never wanted to come near him again. He didn't care if they thought he was some sort of monster; he just wanted to do something. Anything. He had no clue how long he had been here, but it had been too long. He just needed to prove he wasn't done. Wasn't done fighting back.

The heavy door creaked open, and two searchers stepped into the room. Dakota struggled to his feet, letting a waterfall of sculk wash over his face and down his back. He grinned, anger and spite driving his every move. He must have looked genuinely horrifying, purple and blue tendrils masking his features, talons clenching into the dirt. The smaller of the pair, a boy only a little older than him, raised his gun, hands clearly shaking.

That's right. Dakota's mind hissed, satisfaction flickering in his chest. *You're afraid of me. I'm the creature from your nightmares. That means I'm still something. I matter.*

"Nice of you to join me." Dakota chirped, tone both too low and oddly chipper. "I was starting to think you forgot about your favorite little birdy."

The older guard stared at him for a moment, her face muddled with confusion and anger. She was gripping a long switch, sweat dripping down her clear skin.

"Speaking is against protocol," she said, flipping her visor down to mask her gray eyes. "One more infraction, and I will be forced to terminate."

"OH, NO!" he cried in mock panic. "I wouldn't want to break protocol. I forgot I'm just too dumb to remember how to talk. Silly old me."

"I said shut up!" she spat, cracking her whip against the ground.

"Why I never!" Dakota gasped, trying to look as offended as possible. "I thought the Queen was against animal abuse. I don't think you're allowed to treat such a fragile little bird like this."

CRACK! Dakota felt the switch drive into the side of his arm, sculk seeping into the open wound. It burned like all hell, the steady drip of blood leaving a dark puddle on the floor. He smiled up at her, eyes coated in a stream of purple stars.

I'm winning. Dakota thought. *She ran out of words, so she just lashed out. I'm telling her what she doesn't want to hear. Deep down, she knows I'm more than just some monster. She knows I'm right.*

"You better be careful you're not breaking protocol. Killing a person without a cause is a crime," he said, voice steady.

"You're not a person!" she screamed, almost like she was trying to convince herself. "You're not like the rest of us! Don't pretend you're anything more than another freak of nature!"

"You're," Dakota repeated, his quiet chirps full of excitement. You said you're. I'm still real."

~

The throne room was brighter than Dakota's cell. That was about the only improvement he could see. Because now he had to look at the Queen, Mr. Trent, and the Headmaster's ugly faces. He was chained to the floor, which was quite annoying because this was the perfect opportunity to attack everyone he hated in one room.

"Polly wants a cracker?" the Queen taunted, holding a delicate cage. A small dove was asleep behind the golden bars, and Dakota doubted it was a coincidence the little bird matched his feathers perfectly.

"You could have asked for my consent before making me look at something so hideous," Dakota said, flicking some sculk onto the Headmaster's skirt.

"I TOLD YOU TO CONTROL THAT!" the Headmaster snarled, tail lashing dangerously.

I'm sorry," he smirked. I'm just too bird-brained to hear you. But it does look quite lovely. I think the less of you people can see, the prettier you are."

"You must think you're really clever." the Queen spat, clenching her claws around the birdcage. "Such a shame a pretty birdie like you is so mouthy. Your sister would make a much better decoration."

His cocky attitude shifted immediately, the mention of his sister shattering the rest of his resolve. He pulled at the chains, panic exploding in his mind.

"SHE ISN'T YOURS!" Dakota shrieked, voice thick with panic. "YOU CAN'T HAVE HER!"

"Oh, but I will." the Queen purred, stroking the dove like a plaything. "Soon, I'll have all your little friends.

"NO!" Dakota cried, his head so full of rage he could barely think. "YOU CAN'T DO THAT!"

"As for you, I have a lovely little display," the Queen continued, ignoring his screeching. It won't be here till later, but I think it will be the perfect spot for you. Right now, you can share a cell with the other little traitor. There's no point using up so much space on such a little bird."

They can't win! Dakota's thoughts screamed. *They can't get Willow! No, NO, NO!*

~

Dakota hit the stone floor with a sickening thud. This room was even darker than the last, shadows swallowing everything in the dome. He could hear quiet tears echoing off the curved walls, and a slumped figure sat against the stone.

Tempest. Dakota thought, fury building in his chest. *How dare he be sad about this! It's all his fault!*

Dakota lunged at the former searcher, claws tightening around Tempest's neck.

"What were you doing!" Dakota snarled, pinning Tempest against the tearstained ground. "You! You're just like the rest of those awful searchers! DIE! ALL OF YOU NEED TO DIE!"

Tempest didn't say anything; he just went limp with defeat. He was much bigger and could easily kill the Avian right there, but he just lay back, ears flat to his head. His usually furious eyes were red from crying, slitted black pupils shifting to gray spheres.

"You're not even going to fight back?" Dakota spat, Tempest's crimson blood staining his hands. "Don't you know what you've done?"

"Yes," he murmured, the words almost nonexistent. "I ruined everything."

Dakota pulled his hands away, startled into releasing his grip. "What did you say?"

"I said I ruined everything," Tempest said, his words choked by sobs. "I-I really thought they cared about me."

"Do you think I'm gonna listen to your stupid excuses?" Dakota hissed, pushing his claws into Tempest's shoulder.

"No," he replied. "You don't have to. I just think it's time I took some responsibility. Because it's not just the Queen. Every time people like me-" Tempest cut off, words choked by sobs. "Every single searcher in this building is holding up a small piece of her empire, and I think it's time I let go. What I'm trying to say is… I'm sorry."

"Why should I listen!" Dakota growled, more and more blood spilling onto the floor. "Why should I ever listen to you again!"

"You probably shouldn't," Tempest muttered. "I don't really deserve it. I've sent too many friends away, ruined too many lives. I realized how much loyalty I've shown. If this is the consequence, I think it's pretty justified. Eye for an eye, you know?"

Dakota wanted to. It would be so easy. He just had to sink his claws a little deeper, and Tempest would be gone. The world would be better with one less searcher in it. Tempest had done too much. He could have gotten Willow killed! Tempest had tried to murder him! Tempest had helped send Dakota's friends and family away in the name of a tyrant. He could finally start avenging every Avain hurt at a searcher's hand. He was finally in control. And Tempest was completely at his mercy.

No.

Dakota wasn't going to be the demon they wanted him to be.

He let go.

Chapter Sixteen

Willow Orio

Willow's life was collapsing all over again. She could feel it, summer air winding around her wings and soaking through her broken soul. The blue sky felt shattered, steel helicopter blades whirring in her ear. Heavy sobs raked her chest, all the fear and loss coating her thoughts in a thick honey. She was perched on a tree, the only landmark for miles across the empty plains. The field was once full of trees just like it, but the heat had flattened them back into the dusty ground one by one. This was it. The very last one, its gnarled roots latching into the earth, unwilling to let go of life, refusing to join its brothers in the darkness. Rot and decay oozed from the branches, hollow stems sending tremors through the shivering leaves. It was pushing against the dust, branches reaching for the blazing sun. Willow could hear the wind whispering insults, desert spirits betting on its demise. The world was burying it, piling on the sand until it suffocated. Perhaps that's why she couldn't stomach going back to camp. She just didn't want to leave the little tree behind. Sharp needles were stabbing at her, the pain of the dying branches cutting deep into her heart. She could feel the air getting thicker like the sky itself was trying to smother the fragile leaves. Willow just couldn't… leave it here alone. She knew what it was like to be alone, feeling betrayed by the ground you stand on, choking on the air you're supposed to breathe.

He's going to die there. Willow's thoughts murmured, horrific images flashing through her mind. *All alone. I can't be there, and he's all alone. My flock is gone, and everything is wilting, and I hate that I'm scared, but I hate that I'm sad, and I hate that I can't control myself an-*

"Sitting here won't keep the planets from spinning," Nevia said, her calm voice breaking into Willow's thoughts. "You can already feel the splintering cosmos.

"No, it's fine!" Willow squawked, wiping sculk off her wings with panicked motions. "Can you just leave?"

Nevia looked at Willow for a long moment before settling on the branch beside her.

"Go away!" Willow pleaded, desperately pushing back the starry tears welling in her eyes. She wanted to disappear, her small frame shrinking deeper and deeper into her sweater. "Please. Please don't look at me like this."

Nevia was just staring at her, purple liquid reflecting so that her deep blue eyes looked like drops of outer space.

"Go," Willow murmured, face buried in her torn sleeve. "I'm okay."

"You can't wear that mask forever," Nevia said, dragging her finger through the sculk, tiny claws leaving constellations in the bark. "The wind is whispering our secrets to those willing to listen.

"Stop with the stupid riddles!" Willow cried, her shrill voice muffled by fabric. "I don't get it, okay!"

"I think you do," Nevia replied in a steady tone. "You can hear it, you can sense it, I know you can. I can see the stars in your soul. You can feel the future. You can see the spirits. Others thoughts have been dragging you down. You're like me."

"It's not there." Willow murmured, wings pressed firmly against her back. "the voices aren't real. Everyone feels that. They can sense that thickness. I'm just like the rest of them."

"Lying to yourself won't make it go away." Nevia continued. "It's a gift. The constellations have already chosen you."

"I don't want it." Willow sobbed, long hair covering her face in golden waves. "I don't want any power. I don't want to be mocked, laughed at, judged, despised. I want to be like everyone else. I don't want to be just another stupid Avain!"

Willow could feel guilty tears burning in her eyes, the hot liquid quelling in silent self-hatred. She was so frustrated it hurt, all the contradictions jumbling in her thoughts. She hated how different she was, but also hated that she wanted to change. She didn't want to be alone but wouldn't let anyone get too close. She had tried to rid herself of Avian customs, but she would give anything to get her brother back.

"Soon, it's going to be over," Nevia whispered, turning her starry gaze toward the dusty plains. "Soon, this land will be purged of its wicked ruler, and then the tears in our nation will be healed with time."

"What if Dakota never gets to see that?" Willow whispered, her voice choked by the tears she couldn't hold back. "What, what if he's already gone?"

Willow looked up to meet Nevias eyes, silent fears building with every wave of sculk. The seer was holding her arms open, shining eyes so serenely still Willow felt she could get lost in them. And before she could change her mind, she let herself fall into the seer's arms. Willow took down the barriers, letting the sculk flow freely over her wings and arms, heavy sobs raking her chest.

"I want my brother back." Willow choked, wings wrapping Nevia in a tight hug. "I need him to be okay."

"He will be," Nevia whispered. "I promise he will be okay. It's all going to be okay."

Willow hoped she was right.

Chapter Seventeen

Callax Trent

Callax was really starting to get sick of cleaning blood off his prosthetic. In fact, he was done with blood in general. In a perfect world, he would never have to look at it again. But the world wasn't perfect, and Callax could still feel the sticky liquid dripping from his chest and sinking into the dusty floor.

Thanks for this, Uncle. Callax thought wryly. *I hope you got a promotion for your trouble.*

He wished his family was here. Any of them, second cousins, great aunts… his parents. But it was stupid to hope for the impossible. The only family he had left was a psychopathic uncle who committed war crimes for a living. And he doubted seeing him was a good idea.

"You look like someone just killed your dog." Pearl grinned, and Callax noticed her fading eyes were almost completely dry. They looked like a cracked desert floor, veins branching out into dusty wells of spilling red. Her tail was ripped to shreds, no doubt because she lacked the strength to lift it off the ground. Brown hair fell over her shoulders in a tangled mess of sand and blood, her blushed face reminding Callax of a dried rose. Pearl looked… dead.

"Sorry," Callax replied hastily, sitting up to meet her faded gaze. "Just zoned out a bit. Ar-are you sure you're not tired?"

Pearl rolled her eyes, that confident smirk flashing in the pale light. "Have you seen yourself lately? The last thing on your mind should be if your friends are sleepy."

"I guess you're right," Callax murmured.

"I know I'm right." Pearl countered playfully.

"Yeah, yeah," Callax responded, struggling to his feet. "You wanna go get some fresh air? Caves kinda eerie when it's just us."

Pearl whipped around, glancing out the cave entrance before returning to face him. She was twitching violently, and her dull heartbeat was somehow audible, the quiet rhythm echoing through the cave walls.

"YEP." Pearl cried, voice rising like she was trying to talk over someone.

"Are you sure?" Callax asked. "You sound a little… antsy."

She looked down at the dust for a long moment, her shaking limbs getting stiffer with every labored breath. When she glanced back up to meet his eyes, she was smiling like nothing had happened. She was just… fine. Not her body; she still looked dreadful, but her expression was so happy. It was kind of unsettling to see a smile so perfect. It was like she'd planned this, her face almost too genuine to be authentic.

"What did I just tell you?" she chided, jumping to her feet with an overflow of enthusiasm. "Come on! I wanna see the stars!"

~

It was the most beautiful night sky Callax had ever seen. Unfairly beautiful, considering Dakota wouldn't get to see it. He already missed the Avains happy chirping, his insane ideas, just how much he cared. The air was so warm like the sky was wrapping him up in a blanket made of embers. His tail was a flurry of sparks, the heat reminding him of home. His real home, with the steaming forge, his father's smelting filling the house with the scent of metal. His mother playing board games with him, dice stained the color of sunflowers. His cousins running through the orchard, climbing trees until the last of the sun dipped under the clouds. Aunt Rachel scolding him for letting the dogs get the food. It was nice to remember, to pretend this was all some stupid dream. But it wasn't. In dreams, you wake up.

"I-Its nice o-ut." Pearl shuttered, hand twitching slightly. She was lying beside him, tangled hair sprawling in the dry grass.

"Are you cold?" Callax asked, tilting his head to look at her.

She let out a smothered laugh like there was an inside joke he wasn't getting.

"No, it's just… different," she murmured, clutching his hand like a lifeline. "I'm not quite used to it."

"Do you need to go inside?" Callax asked

"No," she replied, closing her eyes and rolling back to face the sky. "I'm happy here. Happy with you."

Callax didn't argue. Despite everything, he was enjoying himself. The weather was perfect, milky air reminding him of everything he had left behind. But not in a regretful kind of way. It was more like being in a good dream. And Pearl was here. Pearl, with her unwavering joy, and unbreakable spirit. He was so glad he wasn't alone. That she, that all of them, chose to stay. He didn't have a family anymore, and that would hurt forever. But he was far from alone. He cared about all of his friends more than he could express. And right now, two of them needed him. Dakota was up there, trapped. And despite Tempest's MANY mistakes, he still came with them. He saved Callax's life, and even unwillingly, it still counted. The fact is, Callax needed to return the favor. He needed to stop being the punching bag for the world and do something.

Pearl's hand stiffened, the contact spilling another drop of crimson blood onto the grass. The makeshift bandage had long since fallen off, leaving Callax's thin shirt the only thing between the gash and open air. Callax lifted his free hand up to his eyes, the thick blood dripping off his fingers onto his scarred cheek. And all he could see was violent red.

The world wasn't perfect. It never would be. But that didn't mean he couldn't try.

He could hear Pearl's heart slowing, her clenched fingers loosening around his hand. She drifted in and out of sleep, her breathing no more than a whisper. She looked so beautiful there in the field. He thought about waking her up to go back inside but decided against it. He wanted to stay here, sinking into the milky air, letting the silent embers quell his pain. Holding her hand, just the two of them on a beautiful night. He lay there, staring up at the stars. They were tinted, crimson ooze filling his eyes and covering the constellations. He was sinking into sleep, warm dreams reaching for him, dragging him into unconsciousness. He could hear whispers, whispers of his parents, Dakota, Tempest, even his Uncle. They were hissing, muttering his hopes… and fears. Suddenly, another voice broke into his dream, cold and mocking. She was cackling, her raspy laugh radiating sick delight. He could hear stomping boots and gunshots denting ancient trees. She only spoke once, but the words seemed to echo forever.

Let's see what you do now, little hero.

Chapter Eighteen

Archimedes Orio

Day 7536
Has it really been that long?
No.
It had been longer.
Longer since the start, anyway.

Archimedes wasn't really sure what the start was anymore.

There was a knock on the steel door, and Archimedes could hear talons scraping against the stone floor. He let out an annoyed chirp, turning to pause his vocal log. He pressed his fingers against the bridge of his nose, smearing sculk against his wrinkled face. His wings were folded back, crumpled feathers in desperate need of preening. A small cake sat on the desk, an unlit candle slipping off the melted icing. It had been dropped off by Griffin earlier that day, a futile attempt to celebrate his 64th birthday. He used to get excited about getting older, but now it seemed almost like a timer. A constant reminder that he might not get to see the new nation they all dreamed of. That he might die before the war even really started. That he would have to leave his flock behind in this half-baked attempt at a rebel movement. And that despite all his efforts, he would never see his son again. Never get to know how his grandchildren looked all grown up. Had Dakota made new friends? Did Willow keep painting? Did they miss him?

"Come in," he chirped, fiddling with the vials on his desk.

"Happy birthday." Wren cooed, placing a kiss in Archimedes' tangled brown hair. She smiled, soft wings wrapping him in a hug.

Archimedes could feel sculk creeping over his wings as happiness flooded his troubled thoughts. Wren's baby blue eyes seemed to go on forever, milky irises perfectly contrasting dark pupils. Her wings were fluffed up, pale face still elegant even in her old age. That shining smile he fell in love with all those years ago, gazing back at him, her gentle reassurance soaking into his aching bones. She was the most beautiful Avian in all of creation, his loving wife, and there was no way he could lead this movement without her.

"Hello darlin." he chirped, running his fingers through her strawberry blonde hair. "Any news?"

"Saw some helicopters fly by about an hour ago," she said nonchalantly.

"How odd," Archimedes said, his expression twisting into a frown. "Why would helicopters be so far out?"

"No clue." she shrugged. "What are you up to?"

"I'm just looking over the castle blueprints," he muttered, pushing away the ripped paper scraps. "I still don't have any ideas."

"Sorry, hon," Wren murmured. "I just don't think we have enough people for a full attack."

Archimedes let out an angry huff, frustration building in his chest. She was right; there was absolutely no way. They had about 20 people in fighting condition. The queen had about 100 times that on patrol at all times. No matter what they did, his squadron would die before reaching the gates. Even after 8 years of planning, he was yet to think of a solution.

"Oh, I forgot," Wren chirped, breaking into his train of thought. "Maple said she needed to speak to you. Apparently, it's really important."

He rose from his desk chair, unfurling his light brown wings. Walking out of the cramped room, he longed for taller ceilings. The ravine had been quickly converted into a shelter, but the stone was unmoving. Living underground got quite depressing, and he often found himself missing the open skies. There was still room to fly, but it wasn't the same. Like the rocks wanted to watch them plummet to the ground. It was a cruel contradiction, the empty center and the strange flying. The ravine had no floor, waterfalls cascading down into the abyss. The cavern was dotted with holes, all leading off into rooms much like his own, the spires of rock holding blankets, tools, and other items shooting out from the void. Avians were perched on the most prominent peaks, gray walls reflecting off the colorful feathers. It was around noon, so the ravine was bustling, people laughing and joking, the smell of fresh food filling the air.

Tiny drops of water were coming off the ceiling and sliding down the spires, making the air thick and humid. He landed on an outcropping leading off into a cave. The room was illuminated by a mechanical glow, handmade weapons hanging from the smooth stone walls. A metal desk was sitting in the corner, the grimy surface covered in an array of broken tools. Maple was hunched over her forge, twitching red tail flicking hot coals. She was so focused, bandana tying up her auburn hair. Long braids tied with colorful string were coming loose from her ponytail, freckled skin bathed in flames. Archimedes puffed up his feathers, pride sending another wave of sculk over his wings. Maple was getting on so well. He had found her 2 years ago, just a girl alone in the world, an entire village destroyed in a desperate attempt to catch a runaway. Maple often talked about old friends, family, and camps she would never go to. She missed it; Archimedes could tell that much.

"You're here!" Maple exclaimed, smothering her fire in one quick movement. "I have something to show you!"

She raced to her forge, pulling out a long golden strand. Pulling out a hunk of gray metal, she wove the golden metal around the edges, adorning it in a flurry of copper sparks. As he looked closer, he noticed it was a shortsword, the most beautiful weapon he had ever seen. The hilt had a nearly dream-like glow, branching off into a strong stone tip. She turned the weapon over in her hand, before handing it to the startled Avian.

"Whaddya think?" she asked cheerfully, rocking back and forth with her hands in her pockets.

"It's beautiful." he breathed, eyes wide. "Is this for me?"

"Yeah, I hope you like it." Maple smiled. "I just thought, well, the king needed a weapon to suit him."

"Oh, I'm not kin-" Archmedies started, being cut off by the scraping of talons entering behind him. He whipped around, spotting a nervous avian with colorful blue wings.

Bluejay. Archimedes thought frustratedly.

"Um…" Bluejay stuttered, stepping into the room with shaking talons. His cyan wings twitched violently, and Archimedes immediately recognized him from the medical division. "Sorry to bother you, sir. I'm getting some weird readings on the surface."

"What kind of readings?" he asked, whipping around to face the nervous Avain.

"I-it a heat signature," Bluejay murmured, his pale eyes fixed on the ground. "Four of them"

"Are you telling me there's people up there?" Archimedes demanded.

"Y-yes," Bluejay replied nervously.

"Are they searchers?" Archimedes asked

"I can't tell. Sorry, sir." Bluejay whispered, his lemon hair masking his features.

"I'll lead a scouting party immediately." Archimedes said

"Is that really a good idea?" Bluejay asked quietly. "What if it's a trap? We heard a helicopter not long ago."

"And what if it's not?" Archimedes demanded. "What if they need help? And we just left them there? What kind of leader would I be?"

"Sir…"

"I'm going," he growled. "Be ready for my leave in 10 minutes."

Chapter Nineteen

Willow Orio

Willow was resting on the hill, wings stretched out to catch the afternoon rays. She saw Callax lying beside her, a smile flickering across his scarred face. Pearl was sitting behind him, braiding tiny flowers into his dusty brown hair. She was grinning, battered tail twitching happily. Nevia was curled up in the dirt, eyes focused on something far away. She was clearly lost in thought, her restless fingers fidgeting with a small acorn, nails digging into the hard shell. It was such a nice day, warm air wrapping around Willow like a blanket. The sky was a pale yellow, clouds bleeding out into sunset spirals. It reminded Willow of a painting, colors so vivid they didn't seem real. The kind of painting that would never fade, pen strokes filled with so much emotion you can't help but get lost in it.

"Ow!" Callax teased, tilting his head to look up at Pearl. "I don't think my hair is long enough for this."

"Nonsense!" she shot back, weaving another purple flower between the leaves. "No one is too good for braids."

"Hmmm," Callax murmured, his tail flicking embers onto the dry ground.

"Just agree with me," Pearl said, plucking at the grass. "It'll save time."

"You're the boss," he replied, closing his eyes.

Willow turned back to face the vibrant sky, happy Pearl was getting on with Callax so well. The only guy Pearl had loved was god awful, and Willow remembered their breakup too clearly. She wasn't sure if they would ever be an actual couple. Pearl had friend-zoned plenty of nice guys before and now was a terrible time to think about high school romance. But it was cute to see them flirt.

She turned back to the sky, trying to imagine her brother was lying beside her. His wings would be wrapped around her shoulder, dusty blonde hair getting in his eyes. She knew it wasn't real, but it was nice to pretend sometimes.

"Willow? Is that you?" a soft voice whispered from behind her.

She scrambled upward, turning to face the person the voice belonged to. The tone sounded familiar, like something she had heard a hundred times before. Something she never expected to hear again.

"Grandpa!" she chirped, flinging herself into his open arms. Sculk was pouring over her face, soaking her sweater like warm honey. She could feel his powerful wings wrapping around her petite frame, his weathered laugh ringing in her ears. He was wearing a thin shirt with only one sleeve and black mesh tucked into his pants. A long strap ran across his back and through his wings, hosting up a wooden bow with bronze accents. The outfit was clearly handmade, and Willow recognized it as traditional. She used to wear something similar to archery practice before the club was shut down, and all her old clothes were banned by the school dress code.

"I missed you so much," Archimedies murmured, stroking her honey-blonde hair. You have no idea how much your grandma and I missed you."

"I thought I'd never see you again," she whispered, letting his strong wings shut out the rest of the world.

"What are you doing all the way out here?" Archimedes asked, pulling away from his granddaughter.

Willow felt her stomach twist, the words dry on her tongue.

"I... Callax," she started, gesturing to the startled Derorian. "He was attacked by the searchers. We had to run... We- were being hunted. And-"

She stopped, voice choked by tears building in her throat.

"Dakotas- he's." she continued, fighting to keep her voice steady. "He's in the capital."

Archimedes froze, face shifting almost instantly. He pulled Willow to his chest, holding her like a little kid again.

"We're going to get him back." Archimedes whispered.

"Sorry to intrude," Nevia said, hands folded in front of her. "But I believe I have vital information. Would you be so kind as to take us to your underground city?"

"How-" Archimedes stuttered, eyes narrowing. "How do you know about that?"

"Answers will come to those who wait," Nevia said, a light smile flickering past her face. "Now, the city?"

~

Willow was sitting on a table, Bluejay's rough fingers sifting through her damaged feathers, checking for injury. His skin was uncomfortably cold, shaking hands scraping against her skin like sandpaper. She wore a plain white shirt, holes hastily cut to fit her wings. The shorts were the same color, with a small gray patch on the bottom. Bluejay had been horrified when he saw the condition of her clothes, and she wouldn't be surprised if he threw out her sweater for good.

"You're done," Bluejay murmured, turning to wash his hands with disinfectant. "Just some minor cuts. Try not to fly for more than 20 minutes at a time.

"Thanks," she replied absently, jumping off the table to stand on the floor.

"Your grandparents need you in the commission room," he said. "It's next to the second spire, near the entrance. You can't miss it."

"She nodded, lifting off the balcony. She could hear whispers, both from the spirits and the people around her. She could spot some of her family through the crowd, aunts, uncles, and cousins she never thought she'd see again. She landed on a rock ledge, the stony floor covered in various animal pelts. Callax was sitting on the edge, a crooked grin pasted on his face. He was wearing a white shirt much like her own, and it was clearly made for Avians. It was small on him, his bony frame sticking out clearly against the fabric. She could see a tight bandage tied around his chest, a light spot of red showing through the tournette. There were holes cut into the back of the shirt, meant large wings.

"Hey, Callax said, struggling to his feet. "You feeling any better?"

"Yeah," she replied. "Did you get your wound looked at yet?"

"Sorta." He tilted his head as if he was unsure what to say. "They bandaged it up, and I got to change clothes, but they don't trust me on the rocks. The doctor's worried I'm gonna die if I try to climb the rope ladder up to the infirmary, either of blood loss or impact. They didn't bother making it safe because they don't care if they fall."

"Sorry." she winced. "That sucks."

"It's fine," he murmured, shrugging. "All it means is that Pearl and I aren't allowed to take showers yet."

"Where is Pearl, anyway?"

"She's in there," Callax answered, pointing towards the cave. "So's Nevia and your grandparents."

"You ready to meet up?" Willow asked, looking up at him.

"I-I'm gonna be honest," Callax exhaled, smile fading. "Not really. I'm scared. Nevia already told them the whole… Prophecy thing, so now it's going to be pretty awkward. I don't

116

really want all the pressure. I'm not cut out for this being a hero thing."

"You might not be ready," Willow chirped, trying to sound reassuring. "But you will try."

"Ready?" she said kindly, helping him to his feet.

"As I'll ever be," he said wryly. "Let's go."

Chapter Twenty

Callax Trent

Callax couldn't help but notice that everyone was staring at him. He could feel eyes burning into his mind, every glace furthering his anxiety. He was sitting at a large circular table, a white sheet draped over the wood. Pearl was next to him, and at least 4 other Avians were at the council. It was a weird feeling to have everyone want something from you. Callax could hear muffled whispers about himself but didn't hear his name once. He was just… the Deroian. It was like he was one of the people in those anonymous internet stories. People knew *of* him, but they didn't know who he was.

"The council will now come to order!" Archimedes declared, clear voice echoing off the walls of the cave. "Who would like to start discussion?"

"I," an Avian woman chirped, her sharp black wings flared wide. She was in her mid-twenties, a long scar snaking down her arm. Does the arrival of the Deroian mean we're finally going to go through with a serious attack?"

"Most likely," Archimedes admitted. "It's definitely a possibility."

"Excuse me, sir," Bluejay stuttered, light cyan feathers twitching nervously. "Are we sure that's wise? We have already established that we are at a large tactical disadvantage. And I think hinging our decision on someone's hallucination would be impulsive and unintelligent."

"It's no hallucination," Nevia smirked. "But if you prefer to stay here indefinitely, alright."

"It's not so bad here," he replied, fixing his eyes on the floor. "What if we gave up on the idea of rebellion? We already have our freedom."

"Are you suggesting we QUIT!" the woman hissed, her black wings flapping wildly. "Do you have any idea how many Avians are still stuck up in those factories?"

"I'm just saying that we shouldn't go off on a suicide mission," he muttered. "Besides, why should we let her ask all the questions? She's always trying to start a fight."

"You would think that." she hissed, black wings flicking dismissively. "There's a reason you head the medical division. I don't think you have the guts for a real battle. Besides, now that we have the Deroian, we can't lose!"

"Are we sure he's really that special?" a middle-aged man argued from the back. He was sprawled over his chair, large red wings folded against his back. His ginger hair was tied in a bun, and the side of his face looked like it had been burnt, skin smooth at the edges. "It sounds like he's just a kid with a target painted on his back."

"He's going to help us." she insisted, digging her talons into the stone. "He will help us, right?"

"Why don't you just ask him?" the man smirked, pointing two fingers at Callax. "I'm sure the little hero can talk."

Callax felt his mouth go dry, heartbeat thudding to a stop. There were so many eyes on him. He felt like he was suffocating, everything he was supposed to say rushing through his mind. He just needed to reassure them. Tell everyone that he was the great hero they were waiting for. The kind of person they write prophecies about. It was on the tip of his tongue, words building in his throat until he couldn't breathe. He opened his mouth to speak, but his voice wouldn't work. He made a choking noise, heroic speech dying on his lips. He couldn't do it. It was all too much. Too much pressure.

"Oh, I guess I was wrong." the ginger Avian scoffed. "At least he's not dishing up false hope."

"You okay?" Pearl asked, her voice no more than a hushed whisper.

"Fi-fine," Callax replied, tone coarse and dry. "I-I'm okay."

"This kid can barely talk." he mocked, vibrant wings flaring behind him. "And were supposed to believe he can destroy an empire? We might as well go back to bed."

"There is *something* this boy can help with." a young man hissed from the back of the room. He had dark brown skin and large earrings dangling like crystals. One gray wing protruded from his back, the other just a tattered mess of feathers.

"Frisk, What are you suggesting?" Archimedes asked, keeping his tone even.

"Well, if we're to believe Nevia, the Queen is trying to get to that one." Frisk responded, pointing at Callax who looked like he was trying hard not to pass out. "This prophecy can't happen without the Deroian, and correct me if I'm wrong, he's the one the Queen wants. So why don't we make her a deal? We give her the boy, and everything goes back to normal. We all get to leave the factories, and come home."

"NO!" Pearl screamed, jumping to her feet and pounding on the table. "ABSOLUTELY NOT!"

"You're not an Avian." Frisk scoffed, turning his head to glare at Pearl. "You're lucky even to be at this council and certainly don't get a say in the matter."

"I think this is a valid solution," Bluejay murmured, his gaze flicking towards Callax. "Besides, he might die from his injuries anyway. If we turn him in, we're saving countless lives."

"Do you really want to save lives with more killing?" Willow asked, brown eyes large and pleading. "Freedom isn't worth morality."

"You would believe that," Frisk growled. "You got to live in the capital. You escaped all this. You don't know what it's like to work for a tyrant, wings being torn apart by machines that want you dead. Waiting every day for a release that never came. I know what the capital does to people. You can't fight it. If you were like the rest of us, you would understand."

"I do understand!" Willow cried, sculk flecking her pale skin. "My brother's stuck up there! I hate the capitol just as much as the rest of you!"

"I know about your brother," he spat, malice laced in his tone. And he deserves a sister who is even trying to save him. Instead, you're sitting here, choosing some stranger's life over your flock. You've given up on him."

Willow snapped her mouth shut, tears building in her milky eyes. Archimedes wrapped her in his wings, casting an assertive glare at Frisk.

"We're not doing that," Archimedes said, voice low and commanding. "No sacrifices, Avian or otherwise, and absolutely no contacting the queen. If she banished us for simply being different, she can't be trusted."

"What's stopping me from doing whatever the hell I want?" Frisk snarled.

"You will respect my authority!"

"I'm not sure if you've heard, old man, but not everyone here respects you," he chirped. And plenty of Avians would be happy to follow me instead."

Archimedes pulled Willow closer, face fixed in a stony expression.

"This council is over!"

~

Callax stared at the cold ground, fingers digging into the side of his prosthetic. He was lost in thought, wishing he was at home. He felt sick, the wound in his side throbbing. The council had ended about 30 minutes ago, but he still hadn't got up the nerve to move. It wasn't like he had a place to go anyway. The lamps were off, and the only light in the room was his tail flicking embers against the stone.

"What are you still doing here?" Pearl asked, hair damp and glossy. She had just gotten out of the shower, tiny liquid beads trickling down her tinted skin. Her eyes looked so alive, shining green emeralds of color glistening in the darkness. She was absolutely stunning, her thin white shirt tucked into her shorts.

"Just thinking," he murmured, standing up to look Pearl in the eyes.

She gripped his hands, fingers fitting with his like puzzle pieces.

"Don't you dare let those weirdos get to you." she pleaded, eyes fixed on him. "I swear, if you try to sacrifice yourself, I will be so annoyed."

She tilted her head, eyes wide and pleading. "You weren't thinking about the council, were you?"

"I was thinking about that," Callax admitted, his tail coiling around the chair. "But now all I can think about is how pretty you look with wet hair,"

Pearl laughed, leaning forward until her face was only inches from his. Callax felt her arms wrapped around his neck, the contact sending shivers down his spine.

"You're not allowed to die yet," she whispered, beautiful emerald eyes staring back at him.

"And why not?" he asked, leaning closer to her damp face.

"Because you haven't had your first kiss."

Pearl pressed her lips against his, dark room illuminated in a flurry of sparks. The world seemed to freeze, all of Callax's anxiety lost in the passion of the moment. He could have stayed that way forever, willing to forget about everything else. When Pearl drew back, Callax couldn't help but smile. She was standing awkwardly with a lopsided grin on her face.

"Am I free to die now?" Callax asked.

"Don't you dare!"

"I'm here to stay," he promised, pulling her back into the hug. "Besides, I have plenty left to live for."

Chapter Twenty-One

Willow Orio

Willow was on her hands and knees, blueprints scrawled across the stone floors. She had been in her grandfather's room since the meeting, staring desperately at the castle layout. It was getting her nowhere, the dark lines staying fixed in their impossible position. She knew she could be more helpful elsewhere, but every time she tried to stand, it felt like guilt was tying her to the ground. It felt like giving up.

The door creaked open, and her grandparents stepped in. Willow looked over her shoulder, hands never leaving the papers.

"Willow, your grandfather, and I need to talk to you," Wren said, shifting her wings to fold back. We found a solution—a way to rescue your brother."

"What!" Willow cried, shooting upwards in a flurry of feathers. "Really?"

Archemedeis picked up the west gate blueprint, straightening out the corners. "Near the dam's edge, the mechanics has a weak spot. I discounted it as impossible, but Maple thinks she can break it. We could then use the map to make our way through the pipes. It's a long shot, but I think we could sneak a group of about six undetected."

"I'm coming!" Willow demanded, wings flaring as wide as they would go. Sculk poured over her face, stinging as it hit her eyes.

"I figured you would say that," Archimedes replied bluntly. "You're already on the list. I'm going to lead the mission, Nevia's going to help navigate and Maple's coming for obvious reasons."

"What about grandma?" Willow asked.

"Sorry, sweetie," Wren murmured, cupping Willows's face in her hands. "Someone's gotta take charge while my husband's gone. I'm the only other person with that kind of authority."

"That's only three." Willow chirped, looking over to face her grandfather. "What about the last two people?"

"That's actually what we need to talk to you about." Archimedes sighed. "That Derorian, your friend I think, needs to come. Preferably, he would give a speech before we leave. God knows we need some hope. We were hoping you could help us talk to him. He's probably a little on edge after a meeting like that."

"I can try." Willow agreed, rolling up her notes. "But your general just tried to have him killed. I wouldn't blame Callax for being reluctant."

"Just try." Wren urged. "We need luck on our side if we want any chance of getting your brother back."

Willow felt her chest compress, heartbeat ringing in her ears. She couldn't bear the thought of failure. If they got caught, death was a given. And that was horrifying. Because death for her meant death for Dakota. It would mean this rebellion was over.

"Get Callax in here," Willow murmured softly.

~

"You needed to see me?"

Callax walked into the room, Pearl's hand wrapped tightly around his. He was limping, the metal of his prosthetic caked in dirt and blood. Pearl looked shockingly bright, the dull gray of her eyes replaced with green so deep it looked like you could swim in them.

"Yeah," Willow responded, long blonde hair covering her eyes. "We need you to help us break into the palace."

Callax's face went pale, candlelight flecking his skin. with sparks. "O-of course I will." he stuttered, shoulders tense. "But I'm not so sure I'm the one you need. There's no proof of this prophecy, anyway."

"Even if it's not." Archimedes started, wings folded back diplomatically. "The people in the city need a morale boost. Having some sort of prophesied hero with us will give them hope that we'll return safe from this mission."

"I'm just some kid," Callax said, wringing his hands together nervously. "I don't think I'm the right person for this."

"They don't have to know that," Archimedes reassured. "You're already seen as a hero. Now you just have to act like one."

"Stop pressuring him!" Pearl hissed, slamming her hand on the table. "You want an injured kid leading a war? He's been through enough! No way am I letting you use him!"

"I'm not trying to use him!" Willow cried, panicked at her friend's hostility. "Dakota needs help."

"You just want your brother back!" she spat. "I'm not going to let him die on a suicide mission! I thought you were better than this!"

"Stop, stop," Callax interjected, brown hair brushed to the side. "Pearl, calm down. I'm not being used. I want to help."

"I'm so glad." Archimedes smiled. "Do you think you could give a speech on our leave?"

"Su-sure," Callax replied.

"I want to go!" Pearl declared. "I'm not staying here!"

"Sorry." Archimedes responded. "We already have six."

"Who?"

"Nevia, Willow, Callax, Maple, me, and Bluejay." Archimedes listed.

"Not Bluejay!" Willow hissed. "He's a coward with no business being in the capital."

"We need his medical skills." Archimedes sighed. "Like Pearl said, it's a long journey. We should have someone in case of injury."

"Pearl can do that," Willow exclaimed. "She can come instead."

"YES!" Pearl cried.

"I would feel better if you stayed here," Callax said, blue eyes sparking like burning ice. "It sounds pretty dangerous."

"And miss all the fun?" Pearl smiled wryly. "No way am I letting you change the world all on your own. I'm coming."

"Then it's decided." Archimedes declared. We leave tonight. Callax, I hope you're ready. Everyone is waiting outside, ready to see what you do next.``

Callax gave a small nod, and one by one the room slowly emptied until Willow was alone, but she wasn't ready to go yet. She lifted a candle, letting the flame bathe the room in golden light. The sparks reflected off the walls, making the sculk on her face look like liquid magma. It was seeping into her feathers, outlining her wings in a honey-like coating. Tears were starting to drip from her eyes simply because they could. Her hands stayed planted firmly at her sides, and Willow let the sculk flood over her face and down her back. Emotions flared, her thoughts all piled up in her head like a stack of teetering rocks. Setting the candle on the ground, she let the sculk sit there, staining her white shirt a shiny blue. She felt exposed, invisible eyes fixed on her. And Willow decided that was okay. Right now she just wanted to cry. She looked down at the blueprints for one last time, but her long hair was getting in the way of her eyes, shutting out her surroundings. She usually liked it, it was her own little curtain she could pull over anytime she needed to be alone. But now frustration was building as the walls she had built for so long covered what she wanted to see.

In a moment of impulse she grabbed a sharp dagger sitting on the desk and ran the blade over her finger. Stealing her resolve, she pulled the curtains of blonde in front of her and raised the blade to the length around her neck. She stood there, knife shaking in her hand for what felt like an eternity. It should have been easy, but she wasn't quite willing to cut off what she had used for so long. It wasn't just hair. It represented the walls she had been surrounded by for years. It was her safety net. But not really. The walls were closing in, choking her breath and keeping her inside. From the outside it was a perfect picture, smoothed over with every brick aligned in pattern. She was dying in here. She was choking on everything that had been keeping her alive but nobody could even see it. She wouldn't let them see. She needed to take down the castle but then what? Willow didn't know if she could risk it. What if taking down the stones didn't free her? What if all it did was show everyone how hurt she really was? She tightened her grip around the blade, trying to look through her thick hair. She couldn't see in front of her face. Her breath was choking. She needed to leave this cage she had wandered into. She couldn't live like this. Blinking hard, she shoved the sharp end of the knife against her hair, the curtains falling down beside her in golden bundles. Her hair was now not even to her shoulders, bunching around her ears and down her neck. It was uneven, her poor cutting job leaving it ragged. It was hideous, choppy and ugly and oh so freeing. Her spine instantly felt better, all the weight dragging her head under suddenly releasing. She drew in a long breath, stretched her wings as wide as they would go, and took a moment to appreciate all that she could see.

Chapter Twenty-Two

Mr. Trent

"What an animal!" Mr. Trent's coworker spat, scrubbing at a spot of sculk dotting her uniform. "I can't believe it's still alive!"

Mr. Trent wrung his hands together, guilt piercing his skull like a bullet. For the past three days, all people were talking about were the prisoners. The night after the capture, His coworkers had taken him out for drinks. It was miserable hearing how the execution had already been planned. The worst part was how happy everyone was. They had played darts, the other generals laughing about that little Avian flying into the helicopter blades. Others sat at the corner table, never touching their drinks or joining the games. Mr. Trent just kept throwing darts, trying to ignore the morbid conversation around him. He had recognized the young searcher before, a Kitsune under the red division. He was a skilled boy, if a little sharp. He looked so content during the helicopter ride, the sleep drug lulling him into a false sense of security.

"I wish I could rip off its wings myself," Caspian muttered, hanging his helmet on the coat rack. "And Tempest has to go too, the little traitor."

The tone made Mr. Trent wince; he remembered just weeks ago Caspian was bragging about how Tempest was one of his top soldiers. Caspian was like a father to the young searcher; the entire castle was his home. Tempest's parents weren't around much, so the red division was like his second family. Now, not one of his former friends had even talked to him. But at least they knew his name. The other hadn't even been regarded as human. Mr. Trent wished he knew the Avian's name. He had only ever heard the boy called monster, bird, animal, it. Nothing to ever suggest they were talking about a person. He had only seen the Avian once, tearing at the net as he lifted off into steel blades. Blood was everywhere, feathers ripped into fluffy shreds. He never stopped screaming. His wrists were rubbed raw, sculk pouring over his face like syrup. His eyes were so mad, the metal restraints the only thing keeping him from attacking everything. But he didn't seem feral. He cared too much to be crazy. Every one of his words felt like a personal attack, and Mr. Trent had to bite his lip to keep himself from defending the honor he didn't have. He had to listen to it the whole ride, the Avian screeching names before asking if the soldiers had already forgotten them. Demanding to know if he even knew whose lives he'd ruined. Screaming that the Avains were real and that Mr. Trent's job wasn't just a game. And the worst part was that the Avian was right. Each name felt personal, the words so full of emotion they couldn't come from an animal. And he wasn't even given the right of a name. He was going to die tomorrow, and people were already bidding on who would get to mount his wings on their wall.

One more day, and then Pollux would have another death on his hands. And Tempest wouldn't be far behind.

"Doesn't someone have to go feed it?" Annex pointed out, unwrapping a pair of sandwiches. "It's been a few days."

"It can starve for all I care!" Caspian snarled, sitting beside Annex with a salty glare.

Mr. Trent swallowed the lump in his throat, glancing at Caspian. "I'll do it."

"Sure, if you want to spend your lunch break fighting off a hungry bird, be my guest." Caspian snorted. "If you're not back in ten minutes I'll send backup. You can never be too careful."

"Okay." Trent replied, tentatively walking out the door. His breath caught in his throat, frustrated at himself for doing this. He could have just stayed in the break room, fell asleep on his desk pretending he couldn't read the paperwork he was signing. He would wake up, and the Avian would be gone. He needed to know his name. He needed to let the little bird know he would still be remembered. Mr. Trent knew that was hypocritical, but it didn't change his mind.

The halls were shining, bright summer skies reflecting through the long rectangular windows. As he descended the stairs to the dungeon, the windows quickly became more sparse. By the time he reached the bottom, it was pitch black, silver bars engulfed by dark tendrils. He couldn't imagine spending an hour down here, let alone days.

It's going to work!" a shrill voice screeched from a cell three doors over. "You're not even trying!"

"Throwing yourself into a door isn't doing anything!" Tempest growled. "I'm saving my brain cells to come up with a viable solution."

"If we both hit the door, it would work!" the other voice chirped angrily.

"Shut up!" Tempest yelled back. "It's not working!"

Trents face planched, fingernails digging into the sandwich tupperware. Sweat trickled down his face as he heard the screeching of the Avain. He stepped up to the iron bars, careful not to get too close.

"I-I brought food." He said, voice shaky.

A snarl tore itself from the Avian's chest, flinging himself into the bars. His talons were wrapped around the metal, hands reaching through the slits.

"YOU KILLED THEM!" the boy shrieked, sculk pouring down his face. "YOU SENT THEM AWAY!

Guilt wrenched at his heart, the Avains purple eyes cutting into his soul. He needed to say something, tell him he was sorry, but the words were stuck in his throat.

"JUST HERE TO STARE?" the Avian snarled. "TO SCARED TO FACE ME? AM I THE DEMON IN YOUR NIGHTMARES? JUST ANOTHER ANIMAL?"

No

The monster everyone had been talking about was nothing more than a kid, 15 at most. His wings were not a prize of war, and his death was no victory. He was small, a huge shirt hanging down to his knees. And he just looked desperate, not feral.

"What's your name?" Mr. Trent blurted, shoving the tupperware into the Avain's clenched hands.

"What?" He demanded, narrow eyes widening slightly. He opened the tupperware and took a bite of the sandwich. "Need a name to put on my grave? Don't pretend you guys care that much."

"The others don't know I'm here," Mr. Trent replied, taking a hesitant step forward. "I just didn't think it was fair. You deserve a name."

"You think if the world was fair I would still be here?" he hissed. "No. I would be at home with my sister. And you would be dead."

The Avain stared at him momentarily, his expression shifting into something he couldn't decipher.

"Dakota," he muttered. "That's my name."

"I get it, you know," Tempest whispered from his place on the floor. "I understand."

"What?" Mr. Trent asked, glancing over at the searcher. He was sitting against the wall, tail tucked behind his paws.

"You wanted to succeed," Tempest said. "And you were scared of what would happen if and when you didn't."

"I'm sorry." He murmured. "I know it's too late for me."

"Yeah, it might be." Tempest conceded. "But you'll never know if you don't try."

Mr. Trent choked, guilt burning in the words he wasn't willing to speak.

"If you're really sorry, you should do something about this." Dakota snarled. "It's not about what you want anymore."

He could almost feel his brother looking over his shoulder, old games of heroism flashing in his memories. He… he really didn't want to die. But Dakota was right. No matter what happened, life or death, he was done being a coward.

"Okay." he sighed. He fumbled with his keys, pulling out the one matching the door. He turned the key into the handle, and the cell door creaked open. Dakota stepped forward, flashing him a ferocious smile.

"Seven doors down there's an entrance into the sewer system." Mr. Trent started, letting the words tumble out of his mouth before he could stop himself. " It leads under the castle, and trails until it empties next to the moat. You can crawl out through there."

Dakota nodded, darting off. Tempest went to follow him, before turning to give Mr. Trent one more smile.

"Thank you." Tempest said earnestly. "I won't forget what you did for us.

And with that, they both disappeared into the dark corridor.

They're gone.

He turned, preparing his lie for when he got back, but Caspian was already loading his gun.

Chapter Twenty-Three

Dakota Orio

What was left of Dakota's wings hovered above the swampy water. Dakota could feel his blood churning, slitted holes above him, letting light peek in. But that wasn't the only thing that could be seen through the gaps. Boots were stomping over his head, angry mutters all around him. His wings ached, but he refused to let his feathers drape across the ground. If just one fell to the floor, it would be like leaving a trail exactly where they were going. Tempest was walking beside him, ducking slightly to fit his tall form in the cylindrical tunnel. Dakota didn't feel claustrophobic, but he was much smaller than Tempest. The former searcher could touch both ends of the tunnel with his arms fully extended, and his ears were flat back to avoid dragging across the ceiling. He wore heavy combat boots with a silver button attached to the shoelace. Dakota had seen a similar marking on other searchers, a variety of metals according to their rank in the force. If he recalled correctly, silver was only three spots under the Queen's personal guards and generals. Dakota never really thought about how much work Tempest put into his rank. What a jerk. Dakota kicked over a splash of water, the muck coating the badge and making it look more like a bronzy wood.

"Careful." Tempest hissed quietly, pulling his large boots away from Dakota. "You're getting mud on me."

"Whoops." Dakota chirped dully, not looking over at the former searcher.

Tempest snorted, keeping his head down and continuing down the tunnels.

A gunshot sounded through the corridor and Tempest completely froze. His eyes widened, ears perking up and scraping the top of the hall.

"Oh…" Tempest whispered, bringing his hands up to cover his mouth. He had come to a dead stop, tail tucked close to his knees.

"Let's go." Dakota hissed, annoyance flickering in his mind. "If they're shooting, they're probably on to us!"

"It was Mr Trent." Tempest continued, lip quivering. "I-I heard his voice cut off. I… I heard my division."

"I don't hear anything," Dakota said. "Come on! We have to go now!"

"I heard it," Tempest responded, tears building in his eyes. "He's dead. He died for us. Don't you care?"

"Sure." Dakota snapped, wishing he could be done with this conversation. Mr. Trent had done more than enough to die for. Dakota definitely didn't want him dead, and he was grateful for the help; he just didn't have time to mourn. Besides, all he could think about right now was getting out of this place.

"He helped us," Tempest murmured. "He didn't deserve for it to end like this."

Dakota snorted, clenching his teeth together. "We have to go. We're so close to being back with our families. To get home."

"This was my home!" Tempest exploded, hands shaking against the cold metal. "This is my family! What am I supposed to do?

"Stop being so loud." Dakota spat. "We don't have time for your petty arguments."

"You're awful, you know that." Tempest snapped. "I haven't seen any empathy from you.

"Oh, and you're so much better?" Dakota snarled, whipping around to face him. "At least I'm not defending murderers."

"They're not murderers!" Tempest insisted. "It's an accident! Every time! People don't know what they're doing!"

"Do you think those words bring people back from the dead?" Dakota started furious tears building in his eyes. "I've gotten boxes shipped to my house filled with items belonging to my flockmates. Sticky notes pasted to the front that simply say factory accident! Not even their name! Just a number. Worker 253, factory accident!"

Tempest looked down at the ground, biting his bottom lip until Dakota could see blood staining his teeth.

"Would you be so indifferent if it was me? Tempest asked.

"I don't have time for this," Dakota muttered, ignoring the question. "If you want to die here with your so-called family, be my guest. I don't care what you do because you clearly haven't chosen your side."

Tempest looked ready to yell back, but a sharp growl cut him off.

"I hear them!" a searcher yelled, boots stomping over Dakota's head. Tempest snapped his mouth shut, panic clear on his face. He reached up, seemingly by instinct, to his left ear but didn't touch it. Dakota started to sprint down the tunnels, Tempest glancing back before racing after him. Tempest easily overtook Dakota but slowed down to let the Avian keep pace with him.

Don't stop for me! Dakota thought angrily. *I don't want your pity or your help!*

"They're in the sewage!" another searcher hissed. "Inform Her Majesty! Mobilize all troops!"

Dakota didn't relent, feathers dropping from his wings like a trail. They would know exactly where they were going, but Dakota couldn't stop it. All he could do was run. Every muscle hurt, blood staining his white feathers a crimson red. He wanted nothing more than to collapse on the ground, letting his battered wings fall to the back of his mind. He couldn't be done, though. Whenever he thought about stopping, another fuse blew out in his brain. Willow was murmuring in his ear, letting him know how alone she was. He could hear a searcher laughing about how pretty a cloak full of feathers would be.

The Queen's words were echoing in his head, saying how he was going to die forgotten, just another monster killed for order, never given a name of his own. He remembered every boy at school egging him on to start fights he could never win. And his teachers telling him he would never amount to anything. Tempest, yelling how he would plummet from the air, wings bound and torn. And everyone would relish his fall. Willow would be all alone.

Probably killed once she was inevitably caught. And that was the scariest thing Dakota could think of. He gritted his teeth, racing down the swampy corridors. He refused to go back to his cage. He would rather bleed out in these tunnels than give the Queen a single ounce of his fear. He wasn't just a monster. No way he was playing the games on her terms.

Dakota squeezed his eyes tight, panic fraying his broken nerves. Suddenly, he slammed into something, pain exploding up his back. A startled cry rang in his ear, vision blurring around the edges. He felt large wings wrapping around him and spotted a glimpse of people behind him. Tempest yelled something, but Dakota couldn't make it out. His eyes were fuzzing up, his head pounding at the impact. He was scooped off the ground, people running all around him. A bullet went through his wing, and he could have sworn he heard a panicked cry from beside him. But not just anybody's chirping. It was his sister, and she was screaming.

Chapter Twenty-Four

Callax Trent

"Dakota!" Willow screamed, wings flaring.

Callax stared down at the little Avian, who had just slammed full force into his grandfather. He looked half dead, wings torn into ragged bundles. His eyes were so full of sculk his pupils were nearly invisible, whites replaced by stars. He blinked, limbs hanging like limp vines. Archimedes instantly pulled Dakota upward, wrapping his large wings around the little Avian until all Callax could see of him were his talons dragging uselessly on the floor. Callax felt his skin prickle, the reality of the situation making him nervous. He was standing straight, careful not to let his tail dip into the swampy water, the damp tunnel smothering his internal fire. It made him feel oddly weary, like he was being buried alive. He glanced over at Maple, who looked like a drunken woman. She was completely drenched from pulling back the panel covering the entrance to the moat. If that's what this water did, Callax wouldn't risk touching it. He hoped he wasn't acting so slurred, but there wasn't much to do about it. His shortsword felt heavy on his back, the decorative sheath digging into his side. He was given it before they left; Archimedes said it was meant to be symbolic. They planned to get in and out, never bump into the Queen at all. But hearing the angry shouts down the sewage corridor made him wish he was given a gun or at least a longer blade.

"There's a group of searchers already on their way," Tempest hissed, his injured ear reopening from all the running. Let's go. We can carry Dakota."

Archimedes nodded, his form still regal and assertive even in the panicked situation. He pulled Dakota over his shoulders like a bag, turning to give Willow a slight glance, seemingly checking if she was doing alright. She looked determined, and other than the sculk lining her wings, she was staying remarkably controlled. Her choppy hair stayed away from her eyes, bunching around her ears like a cluster of springs. Callax could feel his chest compressing, breath catching as he spotted the outline of a searcher behind him coming into focus. Bullets started to whiz by, one of them catching Dakota's limp wings. Pearl grabbed Callax's hand, pulling him forward and breaking off into a sprint. Her face was twisted in a determined smile, the swampy water making her skin a steely gray. Callax didn't let her go, running beside her and after the others.

"We won't make it all the way to the moat," Nevia insisted, pointing down a fork in the tunnel. "Down this way. We can use a ladder and get out the front gate."

The front gate? Callax thought doubtfully. *That's going to be well-guarded.*

He glanced back, another bullet barely missing his arm. Nevia was already directing them down the tunnel, and Callax pushed away his doubts. It was smart to follow someone who could see the future anyway.

He scrambled up the ladder, Pearl right behind him. He pulled her up, and the others were already making a break for the door. Searchers were yelling all around him, and one of them started to lower the gate. It was descending, and Callax panicked. He pushed forward, running with Pearl's hand still clenched in his. Nevia slipped under the gate, Archimedes and Dakota right behind her. Callax saw another bullet pass by, shooting through a lock of Pearl's hair. Tempest ducked under, Willow right behind him. Another bullet, but it wasn't quite a miss. Callax couldn't feel it, but his run was shattered, his prosthetic pierced right below the ankle. He stumbled, hitting the floor. He scrambled up, the gate steadily closing. Pearl skidded to a stop, turning to face him. The exit was just inches away, but the gap was getting smaller and smaller.

"I'll meet you out!" Callax said, pushing Pearl's hand away. "Go!"

She didn't move, and Callax saw the exit shrink even further.

"I'm right behind you!" he insisted, limping forward.

"I won't go!" She hissed, keeping pace with him. "I can't go without you!"

It was almost shut

"I made a promise to you," he murmured. "I'm going to be okay."

He shoved her forward, and Willow reached for her friend's hand. Tempest grabbed the other, and Pearl slipped under just as the gate slammed shut. Callax felt relief flood through him as Pearl disappeared out of sight.

She's okay. Callax thought. *No matter what happens to me, she's going to be alright.*

He saw a dark hallway and started to run. Or limp. He couldn't manage anything more than a stumbled jog, and the searchers were already gaining. Adrenaline pushed him forward, heartbeat pounding in his ear. He skidded to a stop, a large golden door the only thing at the end of the hallway. The dragon carved into the front looked like the spirit of death itself, round eyes made of dark gemstone inset in the skull. It had rubies inset all the way down its neck, lining it almost like blood trailing down from its mouth and horns. It had a crown of silver and gold on its slender head, and it looked like the creature was looking down its snout at you, toying with the idea of snapping your neck. Callax heard a bullet from behind his head, bouncing off the grand door and clattering on the floor.

Well, if it's bulletproof, that was good enough for him. Callax pulled it open, slipping behind the metal as another shot clanged off the door. He slammed it shut, breathing heavily. He heard an angry shout from the outside, and Callax pulled his sword out of the sheath and yanked the holster over his head. The metal looked strong enough, and he shoved it through the door handle, hopefully buying him a little time. He turned to look around the room he had wandered into, spotting large piles of gold and silver surrounding marble tiles and silken sheets. He could barely see the wooden flooring through all the wealth, furniture sticking out of the riches like ships lost at sea. It looked like a dragon's hoard mixed with a person's bedroom, blankets draped over an oak desk. A large crystal chandelier was hanging from the ceiling, but the candles were missing except for one on the left side, which was already dying out. The dull light reflected off the crystal ordainments, giving the room an almost dreamlike glow. There was so much wealth and power tucked away in this room like someone was trying to fill a hole. But whoever it belonged to wouldn't even light it up correctly, all this gold and silver hidden under shadows and sheets.

      Callax heard somebody slam into the door, the sheath rattling against the handles. Callax backed away, scanning the room for a hiding place. He looked behind the bed and spotted a pair of dark eyes staring him down. He went pale, the sword heavy in his clenched hand. Before he even had time to register the situation, the creature lunged forward, slamming into his injured chest and pressing him against the golden coins. Gasping, he tried to shove her off, but the Queen was slowly tightening her clawed fingers around his throat, killing his words as soon as they came. He flailed, slicing her wrist with his shortsword, and she reared back, howling in pain. She glowered at him, tail sending her treasure skitting across the floor. He stumbled up, zipping his blue jacket over his bleeding chest like a second layer of skin. Callax just stared at her, struggling to lean off the wall. Blood was pulsing in his ears, chest throbbing at the unwelcome contact. It was eerily quiet, more of a standoff than a fight. He had played this scene over in his head for nights, praying that when his moment came, he would finally feel like the hero he was meant to be. But he was still just a scared little kid. He fumbled with the sword, hearing the sheath rattle as searchers pressed into the door. She lunged forward, and Callax rolled away as she slammed into a pile of sharp gemstones. Her face cracked with pointed shards, and Callax seized his opportunity to press the sharp end of the sword against her neck. It was so close one move from either of them would be the death of her, and the Queen's furious expression instantly shifted into a coy grin.

"How about we make a deal?" the Queen said, trying to choke out her words without touching the blade. "You don't have to die."

Callax didn't back away, her kind tone making his skin prick.

"You can come work in the palace," the Queen continued, hands tightening around her coins. You can live in riches and luxury for the rest of your life with all the treasure you can dream of!"

"No deals." Callax choked, trying to make his voice sound deep and heroic to no avail. He felt his shirt sticking to his skin, the blood seeping through the thin fabric. The bandage was soaked through, plastered to his body so tightly he wouldn't be surprised if he had to cut it off. The flames in his chest felt smothered by dirt, internal fire burning in his eyes like a flickering candle.

He was right there. Inches from her face. Her heavy breathing echoed in his ear, and his heartbeat pounded in his chest. The weapon shook in his hand, sharp end so close to her neck he would barely have to try.

He stared at her, dark eyes blinking fast. They were so wide, full of panic and anger. Now that he was close up, he realized they were not black but instead a dark blue flecked with sparks. The sharp candlelight reflected off her iris, giving them a white sheen. Looking into her eyes, it was hard to remember all the awful things she had done. She was the worst person on earth, the most deserving of death on the entire planet. But when he was this close, all he could think about was that she was a person. Or had been. He couldn't help but wonder what brought her to this point.

What's wrong with me! His mind hissed. *Why can't you do it!*

He just couldn't stop thinking about her eyes. How, if she died, they would never shut… her life would be over, and it would be his fault. He would be a murderer. Just like her.

He wouldn't let himself become that.

He let his hand slip, the blade lowering for just a second. As soon as the tip left her neck, the color in her eyes vanished, and the irises hardened into dark rock. Her nails tightened around her riches, and she flung a handful of sharp gemstones into Callax's face. He shrieked, the sharp stones cutting into his skin and setting his nerves on fire. He staggered back, feeling his back press against the window. He blinked his eyes open, sword clutched tightly against his chest. She rose to her full height, and with an ear piercing screech she flung herself forward, and by instinct, Callax pointed the blade upward. She gasped, crumpling against his sword, which had gone all the way through her ribs and into her heart. She let out one last choking breath, coughing up a trickle of blood before going completely limp. Her eyes glazed over, mouth wide in a scream she would never finish. Callax dropped the blade, letting her fall onto her mountains of treasure. He could see the tip of the weapon on the other side of her body, entirely impaled by the shortsword. Blood was soaking over her gold, scaly limbs peeking under the wealth like a dragon. Callax could barely breathe, ears ringing. He would have thought that he would have been more triumphant when the moment came, but his head was too full of adrenaline to even think straight. He whipped around, and the sheath was slipping from the door handles. Pain exploded up his limbs, and he did everything he could to stay silent as the searchers poured into the room. Pressing himself against the wall, he braced himself for the end of his story.

Chapter Twenty-Five

Pearl Ashi

"No!" Pearl screamed, throwing herself into the gate. "No…"

She stepped back, eyes pouring tears like a choppy river. She scraped her nails down the wooden gate, the entrance completely unmoving. It was made of entire tree trunks, smoothed over and stuck together until they made significant beveled monuments. They slide right into place, a barrier so imposing nobody would dare challenge it. Large stone pillars rose from the ground like spires, almost glowering down at them with invisible eyes. Pearl barely cared, she couldn't even think past what had just occurred.

Callax had been left behind, and she let it happen.

"Pearl!" Willow hissed, giving her friend a pleading look. "Move!"

Pearl jarred back to reality, stumbling up and letting Willow pull her under shelter. Her friend was bleeding, face twisted in a gruesome expression. Her light blonde hair was rustled with dirt and feathers, making it look almost like a bird nest cupped over her head. Dakota was over Archimedes's shoulder, head lolled uselessly to one side.

"When was the last time Dakota slept?" Archimedes demanded, turning to Tempest. The former searcher was standing stiffly, a mixture of the posture soldiers held during ceremonies and the half-frozen position of fear. His coat was gone, and the long-sleeved black undershirt was torn at the left side.

"He, well, he hasn't," Tempest replied, keeping his back straight. "Not since the capture anyway."

Archmedies mumbled a curse, sculk dripping off his cheek.

"Grandpa, what about his wings?" Willow whispered, reaching for her brother. "We can fix them, right?"

Archimedes pulled Willow close, shaking his head. They looked almost like one person, Willow and Dakota nearly invisible under Archimedes' large wings.

"I'm sorry," he murmured. "He's not ever going to fly again."

Willow blinked, letting a long tear trickle down her face before backing away.

"Alright," Maple said, determination in her glazed eyes. "What's the plan?"

"We have to go back!" Pearl insisted, wringing her hands together. "I'm not leaving without him!"

"Nobody is leaving," Archimedes said firmly. "But we need a way back into the castle."

Nevia looked over, her eyes narrowing like she was looking past them and at something far away. Her dark skin seemed to glow against the blues of her palace uniform. She squeezed her eyes shut before blinking them open completely white. Her pupils were gone, replaced by almost milk-like pools of sight.

"Follow me," she commanded, lips slightly out of sync with the words. Pearl felt a chill go down her spine. Nevia looked like she had fallen from the sky, white stars spilling from her eyes and over her face. Her dark hair was bundled out of view by her headdress, the blue color enunciating her features even clearer. She almost glided over the floor, twisted horns sprouting from her head. Eventually, she stopped beside a stone wall and felt the bricks one by one.

"What are you doing?" Tempest asked, confusion plain on his face.

Nevia turned, a light smile plastered on her face. The white eyes were incredibly unsettling, almost like they were being looked over.

"14 years assisting an effort so taxing leaves you with a copious amount of insider knowledge," Nevia said, shoving her hands against the brick. The wall suddenly creaked open, leaving a stony staircase exposed to the outside.

"Where does it lead?" Pearl asked, hope fluttering in her chest.

"My quarters," Nevia responded, starting up the staircase. "I would use this route after certain scenarios where I needed some tranquility."

Pearl raced up the stairs after her, the seer stopping every few minutes to shut her eyes and do some magic mumbo jumbo Pearl didn't understand.

"He's in the Queen's chambers," Nevia said, stumbling. We can head that direction immediately."

Archimedes nodded, rushing up the stairs. They reached the top, and Nevia held up a hand to bring them to a stop.

"Follow my instructions henceforth," Nevia demanded. This is vital. I'm a powerful member of this palace, and you need to stay close."

"What are you going to do?" Maple asked.

"I'm going to anoint our ruler," Nevia replied simply, " and attempt not to get us killed."

Pearl choked, her casual tone mixed with such heavy words taking her off guard. Get us killed didn't sound too great.

Nevia drew in a breath, blinked twice, and strutted out of the room, her face twisted in a stony expression. Nevia was walking perfectly, hands folded before herself like a diplomat, trying not to offend. Pearl slowly trailed after her, the others following in a tight line. Not a searcher was left down this hall; they seemingly converged into one place. Nevia drew to a stop, looking over a grand golden door. She placed one hand on each handle, swinging them open with a majestic sweeping motion.

All the searchers whipped around except for the eight in the middle, who were aiming their long rifles at a slumped figure in the middle. Pearl barley resisted the urge to run up to Callax and pull him close until nobody hurt them again. He was gasping, a trickle of blood dripping from his cheek. One of the searchers had his hand in the air, clearly waiting to give the signal to shoot. Tempest let out a yelp, panic mixing with joy. His face was twisted in a strange expression as if he couldn't decide if he wanted the middle figure to turn around or stay away from him forever. His back was stiffened until he almost resembled Nevia, standing like a perfect stature.

"Mr. Rincher?" Nevia said, dipping her head in respect. The figure turned, keeping his hand up to indicate a cease-fire.

He nodded, ducking into an abject bow. "We are grateful for your return. I was informed you were killed by the rebels."

"Killing a seer is no easy task," Nevia said simply. "Hold your fire. Sir, I believe this is your son?"

The searcher flipped up his vizor, eyes wide with emotion he didn't dare speak. Searchers were screeching around her, and Pearl squeezed her eyes shut. She could hardly believe they hadn't been shot yet. The one referred to as Mr. Rincher was looking them over like he wasn't quite sure if they were really there. He kept his posture tall, keeping his gaze fixed on Tempest. He looked terrified but almost like a repeated terror. She could almost imagine this driven, workhorse boy standing against the wall, perfectly straight, as he prayed today wouldn't be the day he lost his dream. Nearly a minute passed before Mr. Rincher flipped the visor back down, covering up his mismatched eyes that Tempest had gotten in the same colors.

"I have no son." Mr. Rincher said, voice shaky. "My boy died."

Nevia stared at him, before nodding like she had agreed. Tempest looked crestfallen, but he didn't relax his posture, almost like he was hoping the searcher would change his mind if he just stood a little straighter.

"I must have been mistaken," Nevia said, knowing full well that she was correct. "After all, Her Majesty wouldn't lie about the death of a loved one."

She gestured to the Queen, who was crumpled against the ground like a puppet with cut strings.

"Get on with it." a searcher demanded from the crowd. "Shoot 'em and be done with it!"

Nevia whipped her head around so fast it looked like she was above reality. She glowered at the woman, whose outburst slowly died under Nevia's white eyes.

"We are grateful to you for returning the captives to us." Mr. Rincher said, dipping into another bow. "The Queen's death is a great tragedy, and we shall execute these rebels immediately. I trust you will anoint us a strong new leader."

"Who is he?" Nevia asked, ignoring the conversation around her. She gestured to Callax, who had lifted his head slightly. His eyes were glazed over, mouth half open.

"He is a rebel who assassinated Her Majesty. He committed treason." The searcher replied confidently.

"But who is he?" Nevia asked again.

The room fell silent.

"I'll tell you." Nevia continued. "He is a child. His name is Callax Trent. He appears in my dreams every night, a vision of a shining new era. The Queen's death was a long time coming, and it was no tragedy. She brought the fire down on herself, and what will killing this boy achieve?"

"Her majesty was murdered!" somebody yelled, gun raised in the air.

"He ruined the order!" another screamed.

"Have you ever shot somebody?" Nevia asked, face plain. "If so, I want to know why."

A moment of silence passed before a muffled voice broke out from the crowd.

"Um, because her majesty told me to." the searcher murmured.

"I want you to examine this," Nevia said, tone cracking into something forlorn. She gestured to Archimedes, who folded his wings to show Dakota's battered form. The little Avian's head rolled back like a bowling ball, sculk and blood dripping off his body like a maple tap. His oversized shirt hung like a curtain, covering his knees and hiding his heaving chest.

"This is what becomes of the captives you take." Nevia cried, white eyes almost glowing. "Does he deserve this?"

"He's Avian!" a man hissed, dark eyes glinting. "Rebel scum needed to be swept away."

"He is an Avian." Nevia conceded. "But what makes that wrong? And under that, what else is he? A child. Tell me, which of you wants to hang his wings from the wall now?"

Nobody replied, and Nevia continued speaking.

"Killing this boy will not be a victory." she snapped. "It would be a coward's choice."

"Mr. Rincher, I advise you to really think." Nevia insisted, gesturing to Tempest. "Are you going to take the Queen's word that your son is dead, or do you want to take just one more look. I want all of you to take off your visors and study your surroundings. I've seen the future, and I know that it is bright. I've seen shining halls, a better life for all of you. All it takes is a change. The Queen is dead, and the stars have already decided on a leader for us. Just let me bring him forward."

Mr. Rincher looked down for a long time before twitching his left ear and flipping up his visor. The others did the same, a rapid clicking noise going off as Tempest's father set off his silent command. He took a deep breath and beckoned his son forward. Tempest stepped forward, posture stiff and regal. He looked up at his father, trying to keep his tail from twitching. With one movement, Mr. Rincher pulled his son forward, hands closing over his head. Tempest let out his breath, nerves relaxing as he melted into his father's arms.

"I'm sorry," Tempest murmured, tail swinging back and forth. "I'm not what you wanted. Im disappointing, and I'm not going to rank up, and m-"

"I want you." His father insisted, cutting Tempest off. "Exactly how you are now. Forget the blasted rank."

He pulled out of the hug, letting his son go. He looked back to face Nevia, ears twitching.

"Back away from the captive," Mr. Rincher ordered, making a hand motion to his soldiers. They gave him a doubtful look before stepping away. Pearl didn't even wait for them to fully move before running forward and practically tackling Callax into a hug. He blinked slowly, scrapes and cuts mixing with old scars until Pearl couldn't tell the past wounds from the fresh ones. His breathing was raspy, like the cuts were chopping at his words.

"Don't ever do that again," she whispered, wrapping her arms around his neck. "Please, I thought I lost you."

"I don't break promises," he choked out, half laughing. It's gonna be alright."

"The Queen had no heirs!" a searcher shouted from the crowd. "Who have you chosen to lead us?"

Nevia smiled, eyes shifting back until Pearl could see her pupils peeking through the white.

"Archimedes, come forth," she said. Avian's eyes widened, but he didn't argue. He passed Dakota over to Willow and stepped forward to meet Nevia. A gasp rose up from the crowd, angry mutters mixed with confusion. She swept away the gold and jewels, making a circle of flooring. Archimedes kneeled, Nevia pressing her hands together before placing them onto his shoulders.

She murmured something under her breath before stepping back. Archimedes rose to his full height, wings flaring.

"Presenting, his majesty, King Archimedes," Nevia said, dipping into a sweeping bow.

Nobody followed. Not one searcher was ready to bow to an Avian. It was demeaning, ridiculous, and altogether absurd.

"Long live the king!" somebody shouted from the crowd, and a woman bowed, the people around her following in a sweeping circle.

As people slowly fell to their knees, Pearl only had one thought in her head.

Did I just help change the world?

Chapter Twenty-Six

Dakota Orio

"I don't know if I can get used to this," Dakota muttered to himself, staring at the ground between his feet. Sitting on the bench outside the hospital, he was suddenly insecure about his stature. He had never been worried about his height, but back then, he had a 9 ft wingspan.

Now, he was just...

Small.

And he hated it. He felt lopsided and silly; the constant weight on his back suddenly lifted. The one thing that made being him worth it, and it was gone. He was stuck on the ground. He remembered Willow screaming at the doctors, demanding them to find a better solution, but it was a no-go. That's all he could recal before he was given a pill, and then he woke up hours later in a room smelling of death and disinfectant. His wounds were plastered over in a skin like tape, and the largest strip was covering his back in a smooth coating. He was wearing a plain white shirt, but it was missing the large wing holes that were carved into all of his clothing. His nerves were screaming that he was crushing his wings, the fabric smothering limbs he no longer had. It hurt. He didn't want to spend another second in that room. So he left. The park bench was better, anyway. He kept looking up at the sky, doves flying and chirping like they didn't have a care in the world.

Well, they don't care about anything. They can just fly above it all. Dakota thought, frustration building in his chest. *Great. Now I'm jealous of birds.*

He was so mad; he wanted to tear the city down brick by brick, to hurt everyone the way they hurt him. And that made him feel even worse because that made Tempest right. He was still mad. The Queen was dead, his grandfather was king, and the nightmare was over. But he still couldn't let it go. He wanted the searchers to feel bad, to be haunted by what they had done. But they still had their jobs, status, and they weren't being held accountable. Dakota buried his head in his hands, nails digging into the side of his cheeks. He shifted, arms wrapping around his thin frame. He hated how light he was, only about 45 pounds. Useless.

He looked up, spotting his sister poking her head out of the large hospital doors.

"Dakota!" she chirped, fluttering over to sit beside him. "Why would you scare me like that? You were supposed to stay in the building!"

"Sorry," Dakota muttered halfheartedly. "I just couldn't stay there. It was… I just can't."

"It's okay," she replied, folding her wing around his back.

Dakota was suddenly aware of how much older she looked, large brown eyes calm and understanding. She no longer looked like a little girl, powerful wings folded in a long arc. Her curtains of hair were replaced by messy layers, and sculk was showing like tiny freckles down her neck.

"You don't have to go back if you don't want to," Willow reassured, turning to meet his eyes. "Are you doing okay?"

Dakota scowled at the ground, anger bubbling under his skin like magma.

This is all wrong, He thought. *I'm supposed to be hugging her; I'm supposed to be the strong sibling. She needs me. I'm such a failure.*

"fine." He chirped.

"You're not fine."

"It doesn't matter," he said frustratedly.

Willow's eyes softened, reaching for her brother's hand.

"It does matter." she replied. "I can tell it matters to you. You can talk to me."

Dakota stayed silent, not tearing his eyes from the ground. He just wanted her to…

He wasn't even really sure, actually.

"We're a flock." Willow chirped softly. "Let me take care of you."

"Your hair is so pretty cut short." Dakota choked out, keeping his eyes down. "You, well, you grew up."

"That doesn't mean I dont still need you." Willow reassured, seemingly reading his mind. "But you might need me too. And that's okay. We're a team. Always."

"Why me?" Dakota whispered, his resolve finally cracking under his sister's large eyes.

"I don't know." Willow murmured, wrapping her brother in a hug, her fluffy white wings shutting out the rest of the world. "I am so sorry. I don't know why. You don't deserve this."

Dakota let her wings press against his back, almost like a blanket over his raw skin. Dakota could feel sculk from her hands, like thick syrup on her palms.

"It's not fair," she said, her voice almost silent. I know it's not fair."

Dakota pressed his face against her shirt, letting himself fall away from the rest of the world. At that moment, he was okay being small. At that moment, it was gonna be alright. He was here with his sister, his best friend, the person who would care about him forever. And she wasn't the shy little girl who needed to be guarded anymore. Maybe she never was. But in the here and now, Dakota didn't need wings.

He had been fighting for so long. And now there was nothing left to hate.

It was Willow's turn, with her gentle reassurance and calming voice.

Right now, she could fly for both of them.

~

"Slow down, you're gonna get a brain freeze." Callax said, turning to look at Dakota. The little Avian gave him one of his patented whatcha gonna do about it looks, before biting an entire side off his ice cream cone.

"I'm convinced biting ice cream should be punishable by death." Tempest grumbled, hiding his smile. The bullet hole from way back had sealed over, and he was wearing his capitol uniform. A small bronze badge was stuck to his chest, the words 7th circle engraved into the front. Dakota looked at it with a bit of annoyance mixed with guilt. Tempest had been pardoned on the king's command and allowed back into the searchers program, but his troop leader, Caspian, was bitter. Tempest had to start from the bottom, and Dakota knew how long it took for him to earn the first rank. Most of Tempest's searcher friends were being petty, and Tempest couldn't exactly see them the same way after his capture. Dakota was ready to stay mad at Tempest forever, but he was trying to let go of old anger. Not that Tempest was his favorite person or anything, but they were getting better. Forgiveness can't just be handed, but it could be worked on. And his sister had practically absorbed Tempest back into their friend group with kind words and invites to literally everything.

Pearl leaned against Callaxs shoulder, practically dripping with lakewater. Dakota barely smothered his laugh, Callax trying to both hold his girlfriend and avoid getting wet. Pearl was practically in his lap, and she kept getting water in her sherbert. They had decided to meet up at an ice cream parlor, and Dakota was happy to report it was the brightest place he had ever been. The shop was illuminated with large pink lights coming from the ceiling, and all the booths were coated in a metallic blue color. The parlor walls were a lemon yellow color, pretty light pink polka-dots all down the trim. It was nearly empty, except for a group of soldiers huddled around the high top. Every few seconds they would shoot Dakota a glare, and he would glare right back. Dakota kind of expected everyone to stop hating him once his grandfather was crowned, but Avians seemed just as discriminated against as before. Plenty now lived in the capitol, but just as many stayed away. Not everyone was ready to move on, especially the searchers. Most were just happy to keep their jobs and live peacefully, but there had already been three assassination attempts only a year after the coronation. 11 years of hatred can't just be erased, and if Dakota was honest, he wasn't ready to move on either. He hated the headmaster, and he still wouldn't talk civilly with most of Tempest's troop members. He was working on it, but it was hard to be so un-judgemental.

"Sorry I'm late!" Willow said, pushing the doors open with her left wing. "Nevia lost track of time, and I needed to finish the map."

She pulled over a chair, sitting down beside her brother. Her hair had grown almost to her shoulders, and she had a short braid down the left side. She was wearing a shiny blue shirt tucked into a white skirt, clearly a capitol uniform. She had been training with Nevia ever since her power was awakened, and she looked more like a seer every day. Her brown eyes were getting lighter with every lesson, and her sculk was a paler color than before. She had weaker future sight then Nevia, her visions were more sensory based, but grandfather said she was doing wonderfully.

Dakota sank back into his booth, happiness flooding over his nerves. Seeing them all here made him feel like everything was getting better. And that made no sense! He was broken, wings gone forever. The people here hated him, and his grandfather was being plotted against every day. Dakota could see how much everyone was hurt, as plain as the scars over Callaxs face and the badge on Tempest's chest. And everyone was laughing. The past hurt, and maybe it always would. But part of Dakota thought that was okay. When the past was hard, it made the future all the more beautiful.

Acknowledgements

Me, du, it's the author

Hey! Congrats, you did it! The books over! Haha, I know I'm talking to myself, but when I write I like to imagine there's a little guy sitting next to me listening quietly to my story. And now that it's a real physical book, I guess all you guys are my reading buddies. This was such a journey for me, and it's my first work. It's taught me so much about writing, and I hope to improve even more as I continue to write and pursue art. I'm still young, (14), so there's lots to learn. I would like to thank my dad for proofreading the entire thing with me before publishing. He pointed out a lot of important stuff, and since the book was self edited, he was able to give me an outside perspective. Love you dad! I would also like to shout out my mom, she was so proud of me and all her words were so kind. I would like to thank all four of my younger brothers, Ender Indie Adler and Otto, who cracked jokes all the way through and never failed to make me laugh. They had to listen to the whole thing every car ride while I edited, so I'm glad they were willing to sit through that. I want to thank my friends Ashlee and Alisa for being my support crew. They are the coolest friends a girl can ask for and I love them to pieces. I would like to thank an online friend I knew as eevee. He read the entire book before it went out, and the bits of advice and encouragement meant so much. And lastly, I would like to leave you with this. You may be young, or old, or anything in between that. You have a story to tell. So I encourage you to pick up that pencil, boot up your laptop, and think real hard. This entire story was written on google docs on my school chromebook. It was published through amazon kdp. It's literally held together by duct tape and string. And that's alright. You don't need anything to tell a story but a strong imagination, the drive to create, and most importantly, a dream.

~Ivy Hansen